D1600679

ARTISTS' WIVES

Artists'

ALPHONSE DAUDET

Wives

TRANSLATED BY

LAURA ENSOR

INTRODUCTION BY

OLIVIER BERNIER

TURTLE POINT PRESS

HELEN MARX BOOKS

NEW YORK 2009

CONTENTS

INTRODUCTION

Alphonse Daudet, in the literary Paris of the 1880s, was the most envied of men. His books, best-sellers, one and all, provided him with a vast income. His wife Julia, charming and not untalented herself, looked after him devotedly, and defended him fiercely in the endless internecine wars which rent their many acquaintances. His three children were bright and charming. His country house, at Champrosay, was a large, informal, rambling building, equally suited for work and for hospitality. Just as important, Daudet's friendships caused his colleagues to grind their teeth: from Victor Hugo to Edmond de Goncourt, the Daudet salon knew just how to attract glamour. Yet, in spite of all this Daudet was not a happy man.

There were two good reasons for this unhappiness—one physical, one mental. Like so many other writers, painters and composers, Daudet suffered from syphilis, then an untreatable disease, and by the Eighties the disease had progressed to its tertiary stage. One of its many unpleasant manifestations was a series of highly painful leg

Introduction

cramps, the first sign of oncoming paralysis, which caused Daudet to treat himself with, and become addicted to, morphine. Nor could there be any doubt about the prognosis: Daudet knew that he was a condemned man; and indeed, he died, aged 57, in 1897.

The other reason derived, in part at least, from the first: because he was anxious to provide for his wife and children, he felt compelled—as he admitted to Edmond de Goncourt—to earn as much money as possible. He wrote quickly, and produced novels which were likely to please as broad a section of the public as possible. For an author who prided himself on belonging to the fearless Naturalist school, this was a decided come-down—something his enemies never let him forget. And his enemies were numerous: almost every writer who earned less than he did had good reason to hate him.

As it was, the literary world in Paris was huge, and full of rivalries. Every newspaper—and there were many—had a *feuilleton*, a novel, or sometimes a short story, published in daily installments. Then there were the *chroniques*, in which reviews and gossip were carefully blended, and where nastiness was considered to be an essential ingredient. The result was both abundance and the most intense

Introduction

rivalry, with criticism so personal that it not infrequently ended in a duel.

Publishing itself was diverse, with more houses and more novels published than today. Because the reading public was finite and competition more acute, most novels—Daudet's and Zola's were the exception—brought only tiny sums to their authors. How then to make a living? There were the *chroniques* and other pieces of journalism which only brought in a small income. A real gold mine was the theater: a successful play could make a rich man of its author, and novelists, Daudet among them, frequently turned their novels into plays. The majority of these plays (yes, Daudet's too) failed abysmally and deserved to fail. There was the struggle between the traditional theater—comedies and melodramas—and the newer, modern theater in which classical heroes were replaced by scenes of contemporary life. The old-fashioned theater, when handled by professionals like Victorien Sardou was extremely profitable, but the new theater was very likely to see its plays close after five or six performances.

That Daudet had a great natural talent no one could deny. The impoverished son of a bankrupt manufacturer,

Introduction

who first made a living as the duc de Morny's secretary, Daudet had an ear for believable dialogue, and an acute sense of what people wanted. Some of his novels, the *Rois en Exil* series, for instance, concentrate on just the kind of figures that, today still, sell millions of magazines: dethroned kings and glamorous anarchists have apparently lost none of their interest. Others presented the kind of irresistibly fascinating women the middle-class loved to read about as it sat in its comfortably siren-free environment: both *Sappho* and *L'Arlésienne* were made into operas. Finally there were the comic novels. Tartarin de Tarascon is an irresistible anti-hero: not young, not thin, not brave, not smart, his adventures, grotesque but with a happy ending, make for endlessly entertaining reading.

Still, none of that could be described as revolutionary, barrier-breaking literature; and the fact that Daudet was much more successful among the bourgeoisie than with his peers made him extremely sensitive. People generally considered Zola, the other great best-selling author, to be the leader of Naturalism, that daring and popular school. Those of more delicate tastes might prefer the brief, unimaginative but highly realistic and detailed

Introduction

novels of Edmond de Goncourt. Although Daudet was universally acclaimed as a far better novelist than the popular but endlessly conventional Georges Ohnet, the wound still festered.

Hence *Artists' Wives*. Upon reading these charming, often funny, sometimes tragic stories, who could doubt that the author himself must be an artist, a real artist? Only an artist could understand the poets, painters, and composers whose marital difficulties are the subjects of this book. As we are told again and again that artists cannot be happily married, we forget that Daudet himself, after a fairly wild youth, was living the most bourgeois of lives with the most devoted of wives. In one case, and one only, a hint of reality appears: as the errant wife leaves her poet-lover to return to her conventional, garden-loving husband, it begins to seem that ordinary marriages are, after all, not to be despised; but then the poet was not a real poet, so after all, it doesn't count.

The stories themselves are presented as a series of cases in point: real descriptions of real situations, that all take place in contemporary Paris. They can be classified as belonging—as Daudet so desperately wanted them to be—to the Naturalist School but, in fact, they are nothing if

Introduction

not romantic: the presentation of the artist as a creature apart, different from the rest of mankind, is as unrealistic and unnaturalistic as possible. This may well be Daudet's real secret. Without the power and the lyricism of Zola, without the endless, often finicky, delicacy of Goncourt, Daudet has found a way to be both amusing and touching. He entertains, but with a delicate, lyrical touch; he gives us enough of contemporary life to make us feel, as we turn the last page, that we know a good deal about the Paris of the 1880s. He even makes us feel that we, too, belong to that endlessly glamorous if frequently impoverished milieu in which real artists find their inspiration. And that is quite enough to make of *Artists' Wives* just what Daudet wanted it to be: a light and thoroughly enjoyable read.

ARTISTS' WIVES

PROLOGUE

Stretched at full length, on the great divan of a studio, cigars in mouths, two friends—a poet and a painter— were talking together one evening after dinner.

It was the hour of confidences and effusion. The lamp burned softly beneath its shade, limiting its circle of light to the intimacy of the conversation, leaving scarcely distinct the capricious luxury of the vast walls, cumbered with canvases, hangings, panoplies, surmounted by a glass roof through which the somber blue shades of the night penetrated unhindered. The portrait of a woman, leaning slightly forward, as if to listen, alone stood out a little from the shadow; young with intelligent eyes, a grave and sweet mouth and a *spirituel* smile which seemed to defend the husband's easel from fools and disparagers. A low chair pushed away from the fire, two little blue shoes lying on the carpet, indicated also the presence of a child in the house; and indeed from the next room, within which mother and child had but just disappeared, came occasional bursts of soft laughter, of childish babble; the pretty

1

Prologue

flutterings of a nest going off to sleep. All this shed over the artistic interior a vague perfume of family happiness which the poet breathed in with delight.

"Decidedly, my dear fellow," he said to his friend, "you were in the right. There are no two ways of being happy. Happiness lies in this and in nothing else. You must find me a wife."

THE PAINTER
Good Heavens, no! not on my account. Find one for yourself, if you are bent upon it. As for me, I will have nothing to do with it.

THE POET
And why?

THE PAINTER
Because—because artists ought never to marry.

THE POET
That's rather too good. You dare to say that, and the lamp does not go out suddenly, and the walls don't fall down upon your head! But just think, wretch, that for two hours past, you have been setting before me the enviable

Prologue

spectacle of the very happiness you forbid me. Are you by chance like those odious millionaires whose well-being is increased by the sufferings of others, and who better enjoy their own fireside when they reflect that it is raining out of doors, and that there are plenty of poor devils without shelter?

THE PAINTER

Think of me what you will. I have too much affection for you to help you to commit a folly—an irreparable folly.

THE POET

Come! What is it? You are not satisfied? And yet it seems to me that one breathes in happiness here, just as freely as one does air of heaven at a country window.

THE PAINTER

You are right. I am happy, completely happy. I love my wife with all my heart. When I think of my child, I laugh aloud to myself with pleasure. Marriage for me has been a harbour of calm and safe waters, not one in which you make fast to a ring on the shore, at the risk of rusting there for ever, but one of those blue creeks where sails and masts are repaired for fresh excursions into unknown

Prologue

countries. I never worked as well as I have since my marriage. All my best pictures date from then.

THE POET

Well then!

THE PAINTER

My dear fellow, at the risk of seeming a coxcomb, I will say that I look upon my happiness as a kind of miracle, something abnormal and exceptional. Yes! The more I see what marriage is, the more I look back with terror at the risk I ran. I am like those who, ignorant of the dangers they have unwittingly gone through, turn pale when all is over, aroused at their own audacity.

THE POET

But what then are these terrible dangers?

THE PAINTER

The first and greatest of all, is the loss or degradation of one's talent. This should count, I think, with an artist. For observe that at this moment, I am not speaking of the ordinary conditions of life. I grant you, that in general marriage is an excellent thing, and that the majority of men only begin to be of some account when the fam-

Prologue

ily circle completes them or makes them greater. Often, indeed, it is necessary to a profession. A bachelor lawyer cannot even be imagined. He would not have the needful air of weight and gravity. But for all of us, painters, poets, sculptors, musicians, who live outside of life, wholly occupied with studying it, in reproducing it, holding ourselves always a little remote from it, as one steps back from a picture the better to see it, I say that marriage can only be the exception. To that nervous, exacting, impressionable being, that child-man that we call an artist, a special type of woman, almost impossible to find, is needful, and the safest thing to do is not to look for her. Ah! How well our great Delacroix, whom you admire so much, understood that! What a fine existence was his, bounded by his studio wall, devoted exclusively to Art! I was looking the other days at his cottage at Champrosay and the prim little garden full of roses, where he sauntered alone for twenty years! It has the calm and narrowness of celibacy. Well now! Think for a moment of Delacroix married, father of a family, with all the preoccupations of children to bring up, of money matters, of illnesses; do you believe his work would have been the same?

Prologue

You cite Delacroix, I reply Victor Hugo. Do you think that marriage hampered him for instance, while writing so many admirable books?

I think as a matter of fact, that marriage did not hamper him in anything. But all husbands have not the genius that obtains pardon, nor a halo of glory with which to dry the tears they cause to flow. It cannot be very amusing to be the wife of a genius. There are plenty of labourers' wives who are happier.

A curious thing, all the same, this special pleading against marriage, by a married man, who is happy in being so.

I repeat that I don't give myself as an example. My opinion is formed by all the sad things I have seen elsewhere; all the misunderstandings so frequent in the households of artists, and caused solely by their abnormal life. Look at that sculptor who, in full maturity of age and talent, has just exiled himself, leaving wife and children behind

Prologue

him. Public opinion condemns him, and certainly I offer
no excuse for him. And, nevertheless, I can well understand how he arrived at such a point! Here was a fellow
who adored his art, and had a horror of the world, and
society. The wife, though amiable and intelligent, instead
of shielding him from the social obligations he loathed,
condemned him for some ten years to all the exactions
they involved. Thus she induced him to undertake a lot
of official busts, horrible respectabilities in velvet skull
caps, frights of women utterly devoid of grace; she disturbed him ten times a day with importunate visitors, and
then every evening laid out for him a dress suit and light
gloves, and dragged him from drawing-room to drawing-
room. You could tell me he could have replied point-
blank: "No!" But don't you know that the very fact of
our sedentary existences leaves us more than other men
dependent on domestic influence? The atmosphere of the
home envelops us, and if some touch of the ideal does not
lighten it, soon wearies and drags us down. Moreover,
the artist as a rule puts what force and energy he has into
his work, and after his solitary and patient struggles, finds
himself left with not will to oppose to the petty importu-
nities of life. With him, feminine tyrannies have free play.

Prologue

No one is more easily conquered and subdued. Only, beware! He must not be made to feel the yoke too heavily. If one day the invisible bonds with which he is surreptitiously fettered are drawn too tight and arrest the artistic effort, he will all at once tear them asunder, and mistrusting his own weakness, will fly like our sculptor, over the hills and far away.

The wife of this sculptor was astounded at his flight. The unhappy creature is still wondering: "What can I have done to him?" Nothing. She simply did not understand him. For it is not enough to be good and intelligent to be the true helpmate of an artist. A woman must also possess infinite tact, smiling abnegation; and all this is found only by a miracle in a young creature, curious though ignorant as regards life. She is pretty, she has married a well-known man, received everywhere; why should she not wish to show herself a little on his arm? Is it not quite natural? The husband, on the contrary, growing intolerant of society as his talent progresses, finding time short, and art engrossing, refuses to be exhibited. Behold them both miserable, and whether the man gives in or resists, his life is henceforth turned from its course, and from its tranquility. Ah! how many of these ill-matched

Prologue

couples have I known, where the wife was sometimes executioner, sometimes victim, but more often executioner,
and nearly always unwittingly so! The other evening I
was at Dargenty's, the musician. There were but a few
guests, and he was asked to play. Hardly had he begun
one of those pretty mazurkas with a Polish rhythm, which
make him the successor of Chopin, when his wife began
to talk, quite low at first, then a little louder. By degrees
the fire of conversation spread. At the end of a minute I
was the only listener. Then he shut the piano, and said to
me with a heart-rent smile: "It is always like this here—
my wife does not care for music." Can you imagine anything more terrible than to marry a woman who does not
care for your art? Take my word for it, my friend, and
don't marry. You are alone, you are free; keep as precious
things, your liberty and your loneliness.

THE POET

That is all very well! You talk at your ease of solitude.
Presently, when I am gone, if some idea occurs to you,
you will gently follow it by the side of your dying embers,
without feeling around you that atmosphere of isolation,
so vast, so empty, that in it inspiration evaporates and dis-

Prologue

perses. And one may yet bear to be alone in the hours of work; but there are moments of discouragement and weariness, when one doubts oneself, one's art even. That is the moment when it must be happiness to find a faithful and loving heart, ever ready to sympathize with one's depression, to which one may appeal without fearing to disconcert a confidence and enthusiasm that are, in fact, unalterable. And then the child. That sweet unconscious baby smile, is not that the best moral rejuvenescence one can have? Ah! I have often thought over that. For us artists, vain as all must be who live by success, by that superficial esteem, capricious and fleeting, that we call the vogue; for us, above all others, children are indispensable. They alone can console us for growing old. All that we lose, the child gains. The success we have missed, we think: "He will have it," and in proportion as our hair grows thin, we have the joy of seeing it grow again, curly, golden, full of life, on a little fair head at our side.

THE PAINTER

Ah, poet! Poet! Have you thought also of all the mouthfuls which with the end of pen or brush we must nourish a brood?

Prologue

THE POET

Well! Say what you like, the artist is made for family life, and that is so true, that those among us who do not marry, take refuge in temporary relationships, like travelers who, tired of being always homeless, end by settling in a room in some hotel, and pass their lives under the hackneyed notice of the signboard: "Apartments by the month or night."

THE PAINTER

Such are all in the wrong. They accept the worries of wedlock and will never know its joys.

THE POET

You acknowledge then that there are some joys?

Here the painter, instead of replying, rose, searched out from among drawings and sketches a much-thumbed manuscript, and returning to his companion:

"We might argue like this," he said, "for ever so long without either convincing the other. But since notwithstanding my observations, you seem determined to try marriage, here is a little work I beg you to read. It is written—I would have you note—by a married man, much

11

Prologue

in love with his wife, very happy in his home, an observer who, spending his life among artists, amused himself by sketching one or two such households as I spoke of just now. From the first to the last line of this book, all is true, so true that the author would never publish it. Read it, and come to me when you have read it. I think you will have changed your mind."

The poet took the manuscript and carried it home with him; but he did not keep the little book with all the needful care, for I have been able to detach a few leaves from it and boldly offer them to the public.

MADAME HEURTEBISE

She was certainly not intended for an artist's wife, above all for such an artist as this outrageous fellow, impassioned, uproarious and exuberant, who, with his nose in the air and bristling moustaches, rushed through life defiantly flaunting the eccentric and whirlwind-like name of Heurtebise,★ like a challenge thrown down to all the absurd conventionalities and prejudices of the bourgeois class. How, and by what strange charm had the little woman, brought up in a jeweller's shop, behind rows of watch chains and strings of rings, found the means of captivating this poet?

Picture to yourself the affected graces of a shopwoman with insignificant features, cold and ever-smiling eyes, complacent and placid physiognomy, devoid of real elegance, but having a certain love for glitter and tinsel, no doubt caught at her father's shop window, making her take her pleasure in many-coloured satin bows, sashes

★ Hit the blast (literally).

Madame Heurtebise

and buckles; and her hair glossy with cosmetic, stiffly arranged by the hairdresser over the small, obstinate, narrow forehead, where the total absence of wrinkles told less of youth than of complete lack of thought. Such as she was, however, Heurtebise loved and wooed her, and as he happened to possess a small income found no difficulty in winning her.

What pleased her in this marriage was the idea of wedding an author, a well-known man, who would take her to the theatre as often as she wished. As for him, I verily believe that her sham elegance born of the shop, her pretentious manners, pursed-up mouth, and affectedly uplifted little finger fascinated him and appeared to him the height of Parisian refinement; for he was born a peasant and in spite of his intelligence remained one to the end of his days.

Tempted by a quiet happiness and the family life of which he had been so long deprived, Heurtebise spent two years far from his friends, buried in the country, or in out-of-the-way suburban nooks, within easy distance of that great city Paris, which overexcited him even while he yet sought its attenuated atmosphere, just like those invalids who are recommended sea air, but who, too deli-

Madame Heurtebise

cate to bear it in all its strength, are compelled to inhale it from a distance of some miles. From time to time, his name appeared in a newspaper or magazine at the end of an article; but already the freshness of style, the bursts of eloquence, were lacking by which he had been formerly known. We thought: "He is too happy! His happiness has spoilt him."

However, one day he returned amongst us, and we immediately saw that he was not happy. His pallid countenance, drawn features contracted by a perpetual irritability, the violent manners degenerated into a nervous rage, the hollow sound of his once fine ringing laugh, all showed that he was an altered man. Too proud to admit that he had made a mistake, he would not complain, but the old friends who gathered round him were soon convinced that he had made a most foolish marriage, and that henceforth his life must prove a failure. On the other hand, Madame Heurtebise appeared to us, after two years of married life, exactly the same as we had beheld her in the vestry on her wedding day. She wore the same calm and simpering smile, she had as much as ever the air of a shopwoman in her Sunday clothes, only she had gained self-possession. She talked now. In the midst of artistic

Madame Heurtebise

discussions into which Heurtebise passionately threw himself with arbitrary assertions, brutal contempt, or blind enthusiasm, the false and honeyed voice of his wife would suddenly make irruption, forcing him to listen to some idle reasoning or foolish observation invariably outside the subject of discussion. Embarrassed and worried, he would cast us an imploring glance, and strive to resume the interrupted conversation. Then at last, wearied out by her familiar and constant contradiction, by the silliness of her birdlike brain, inflated and empty as any cracknel, he held his tongue, and silently resigned himself to let her go on to the bitter end. But this determined silence exasperated Madame, seemed to her more insulting, more disdainful than anything. Her sharp voice became discordant, and growing higher and shriller, stung and buzzed, like the ceaseless teasing of a fly, till at last her enraged husband in his turn burst out brutal and terrific.

She emerged from these incessant quarrels, which always ended in tears, rested and refreshed, as a lawn after a watering, but he remained broken, fevered, incapable of work. Little by little his very violence was worn out. One evening when I was present at one of these odious scenes, as Madame Heurtebise triumphantly left the

Madame Heurtebise

table, I saw on her husband's face bent downwards during the quarrel and now upraised, an expression of scorn and anger that no words could any longer express. The little woman went off shutting the door with a sharp snap, and he, flushed, with his eyes full of tears, and his mouth distorted by an ironical and despairing smile, made like any school-boy behind his master's back, an atrocious gesture of mingled rage and pain. After a few moments, I heard him murmur, in a voice strangled by emotion: "Ah, if it were not for the child, how I would be off at once!"

For they had a child, a poor little fellow, handsome and dirty, who crawled all over the place, played with dogs bigger than himself, with the spiders in the garden, and made mud-pies. His mother only noticed him to declare him "disgusting" and regret that she had not put him out to nurse. She clung in fact to all the little shopkeeper traditions of her youth, and the untidy home in which she went about from early morn in elaborate costumes and astonishingly dressed hair, recalled the back-shops so dear to her heart, rooms black with filth and want of air, where in the short intervals of rest from commerical life, badly cooked meals were hurriedly eaten, at a bare wooden table, listening all the while for the tinkle of the

Madame Heurtebise

shop-bell. With this class nothing has importance but the street, the street with its passing purchasers and idlers, and its overflowing holiday crowd, that on Sundays throng the sidewalks and pavements. And how bored she was, wretched creature, in the country, how she missed the Paris life! Heurtebise, on the contrary, required the country for his mental health. Paris still bewildered him like some countrified boor on his first visit. His wife could not understand it, and bitterly complained of her exile. By way of diversion she invited her old acquaintances, and when her husband was absent they amused themselves by turning over his papers, his memoranda, and the work he was engaged upon.

"Do look, my dear, how funny it is. He shuts himself up to write this. He paces up and down talking to himself. As for me, I understand nothing of what he does."

And then came endless regrets, and recollections of her past life.

"Ah, if I had known. When I think that I might have married Abertot and Fajon, the linedrapers." She always spoke of the two partners at the same time, as though she would have married the firm. Neither did she restrain her feelings in her husband's work, settling down with her friends in the very room he was writing in, and filling it

Madame Heurtebise

with the silly chatter of idle women, who talked loud, full of disdain for a literary profession which brought in so little and whose most laborious hours always resemble a capricious idleness.

From time to time Heurtebise strove to escape from the life which he felt was daily becoming more dismal. He rushed off to Paris, hired a small room at an hotel, tried to fancy he was a bachelor; but suddenly he thought of his son, and with a desperate longing to embrace him hurried back the same evening into the country. On these occasions, in order to avoid the inevitable scene on his return, he took a friend back with him and kept him there as long as he could. As soon as he was no longer alone face to face with his wife, his fine intellect awoke and his interrupted schemes of work little by little and one after the other came back to him. But what anguish it was when his friends left! He would have kept his guests for ever, clinging to them by all the strength of his ennui. With what sadness would he accompany us to the stand of the little suburban omnibus which bore us back to Paris! and when we left, how slowly he turned homewards over the dusty road, with rounded shoulders and listless arms, listening to the vanishing wheels.

In truth their tête-à-tête life had become unbearable,

Madame Heurtebise

and to avoid it, he tried always to keep his house full. With his easy good-nature, his weariness and indifference, he was soon surrounded by a lot of literary starvelings. A set of scribblers, lazy, cracked day-dreamers, settled down upon him and became more at home than himself; and as his wife was but a fool, incapable of judging, because they talked more loudly, she found them charming and very superior to her husband. The days were spent in idle discussions. There was a clash of empty words, a firing of smallest shot, and poor Heurtebise, motionless and silent in the midst of the tumult, merely smiled and shrugged his shoulders. Sometimes, however, towards the end of an interminable repast, when all his guests, elbows on the table, began around the brandy flasks one of those lengthy maundering conversations, benumbing the clouds of tobacco smoke, an immense feeling of disgust would seize hold of him, and not having the courage to turn out all these poor wretches, he would himself disappear and remain absent for a week.

"My house is full of imbeciles," he said one day to me. "I dare not return." With this kind of existence, he no longer wrote. His name was never seen, and his fortune, squandered in a perpetual craving to have people in

Madame Heurtebise

his house, disappeared in the outstretched hands around him.

It was a long time since we had met when I received one morning a line of his dear little handwriting, formerly so firm, now trembling and uncertain. "We are in Paris. Come and see me. I am so dull." I found him with his wife, his child and his dogs, in a lugubrious little apartment in the Batignolles. The disorder, which in this narrow space could not be spread about, seemed more hideous even than in the country. While the child and dogs rolled about in rooms the size of a chessboard compartment, Heurtebise, who was ill, lay with his face to the wall, in a state of utter prostration. His wife, dressed out as usual, and ever placid, hardly looked at him. "I don't know what is the matter with him," she said to me with a gesture of indifference. On seeing me he had for a moment a return of gaiety, and a minute of his old hearty laugh, but it was soon stifled. As they had kept up in Paris all their suburban habits, there appeared at the breakfast hour, in the midst of this household disorganized by poverty and illness, a parasite, a seedy looking little bald man, cranky and peevish, of whom they always spoke as "the man who has read Proudhon." It was thus that Heurtebise, who

Madame Heurtebise

probably had never known his name, introduced him to
everybody. When he was asked "Who is that?" he un–
hesitatingly replied, "Oh! A very clever fellow, who has
thoroughly studied Proudhon." His knowledge was cer–
tainly not very apparent, for this deep thinker rarely made
himself heard except to complain at table of an ill–cooked
roast or a spoilt sauce. On this occasion, the man who had
read Proudhon declared that the breakfast was detestable,
which however did not prevent his devouring the larger
half of it himself.

How long and lugubrious this meal by the bedside of
my sick friend appeared to me! The wife gossiped as usual,
with a tap now and then to the child, a bone to the dogs,
and a smile to the philosopher, Not once did Heurtebise
turn towards us, and yet he was not asleep. I hardly know
whether he thought. Dear, valiant fellow! In those paltry
and ceaseless struggles, the mainspring of his strong nature
had broken, and he was already beginning to die. The
silent death agony, which however was rather an aban–
donment of life, lasted several months; and then Madame
Heurtebise found herself a widow. Then, as no tears had
dimmed her clear eyes, as she always bestowed the same
care on her glossy locks, and as Abertot and Fajon were

Madame Heurtebise

still available, she married Abertot, perhaps it was Fajon, perhaps even both of them. In any case, she was able to resume the life she was fitted for, and the voluble gossip and eternal smile of the shopwoman.

THE CREDO OF LOVE

To be the wife of a poet! That had been the dream of her life! But ruthless fate, instead of the romantic and fevered existence she sighed for, had doomed her to a peaceful, humdrum happiness, and married her to a rich man at Auteuil, gentle and amiable, perhaps indeed a trifle old for her, possessed of but one passion, perfectly inoffensive and unexciting—that of horticulture. This excellent man spent his days pruning, scissors in hand, tending and trimming a magnificent collection of rose trees, heating a greenhouse, watering flower beds; and really it must be admitted that, for a poor little heart hungering after an ideal, this was hardly sufficient food. Nevertheless for ten years her life remained straightforward and uniform, like the smooth sanded paths in her husband's garden and she pursued it with measured steps, listening with resigned weariness to the dry and irritating sound of the ever-moving scissors, or of the monotonous and endless showers that fell from the watering pots on to the leafy shrubs. The rabid horticulturist bestowed on his

The Credo of Love

wife the same scrupulous attention he gave to his flowers. He carefully regulated the temperature of the drawing-room, overcrowded with nosegays, fearing for her the April frosts or the March sun; and like the plants in pots that are put out and taken in at stated times, he made her live methodically, ever watchful of a change of barometer or phase of the moon.

She remained like this for a long time, closed in by the four walls of the conjugal garden, innocent as clematis, full however of wild aspirations toward other gardens, less staid, less humdrum, where the rose trees would fling out their branches untrained, and the wild growth of weed and briar be taller than the trees, and blossom with unknown and fantastic flowers, luxuriantly coloured by a warmer sun. Such gardens are rarely found save in the books of poets, and so she read many verses, all unknown to the nurseryman, who knew no other poetry than a few almanac distichs such as:

> Quand il pleaut à la Saint-Medard
> Il pleut quarante jours plus tard.

At haphazard, the unfortunate creature ravenously devoured the paltriest rhymes, satisfied if she found in them

The Credo of Love

lines ending in "love" and "passions"; then closing the book, she would spend hours dreaming and sighing: "That would have been the husband for me!"

It is probable that all this would have remained in a state of vague aspiration, if at the terrible age of thirty, which seems to be the decisive critical moment for woman's virtue, as twelve o'clock is for the day's beauty, the irresistible Amaury had not chanced to cross her path. Amaury was a drawing-room poet, one of those fanatics in dress coat and grey kid gloves, who between ten o'clock and midnight go and recite to the world their ecstacies of love, their raptures, their despair, leaning mournfully against the mantelpiece, in the blaze of the lights, while seated around him women, in full evening dress, listen entranced behind their fans.

This one might pose as the very ideal of his kind; with his vulgar but irresistible countenance, sunken eye, pallid complexion, hair cut short and moustaches stiffly plastered with cosmetic. A desperate man such as women love, hopeless of life but irreproachably dressed, a lyric enthusiast, chilled and disheartened, in whom the madness of inspiration can be divined only in the loose and neglected tie of his cravat. But also what success awaits

The Credo of Love

him, when he delivers in a strident voice a tirade from a poem, the *Credo of Love*, more especially the one ending in this extraordinary line:

Moi, je crois à l'amour comme je crois en Dieu!★

Mark you, I strongly suspect the rascal cares as little for God, as for the rest; but women do not look so closely. They are easily caught by a birdlime of words, and every time Amaury recites his *Credo of Love*, you are certain to see all round the drawing-room rows upon rows of little rosy mouths, eagerly opening, ready to swallow the bait of mawkish sentimentality. Just fancy! A poet who has such beautiful moustaches and who believes in love as he believes in God.

For the nurseryman's wife this proved indeed irresistible. In three sittings she was conquered. Only, as at the bottom of this elegiac nature there was some honesty and pride, she would not stoop to any paltry fault. Moreover the poet himself declared in his *Credo* that he only understood one way of erring: that which was openly declared and ready to defy both law and society. Taking therefore

----

★ I believe in love as I believe in God.

The Credo of Love

the *Credo of Love* for her guide, the young woman one
fine day escaped from the garden at Auteuil and went off
to throw herself into her poet's arms.—"I can no longer
live with that man! Take me away!" In such cases the husband is always *that man*, even when he is a horticulturist.

For a moment Amaury was staggered. How on earth
could he have imagined that an ordinary little housewife
of thirty would have taken in earnest a love poem, and
followed it out literally? However he put the best face
he could on his over-good fortune, and as the lady had,
thanks to her little Auteuil garden, remained fresh and
pretty, he carried her off without a murmur. The first days,
all was delightful. They feared lest the husband should
track them. They thought it was advisable to hide under
fictitious names, change hotels, inhabit the most remote
quarters of the town, the surburbs of Paris, the outlying
districts. In the evening they stealthily sallied forth and
took sentimental walks along the fortifications. Oh the
wonderful power of romance! The more she was alarmed,
the more precautions, window blinds and lowered veils,
were necessary, the greater did her poet seem. At night,
they opened the little window of their room and gazing
at the stars rising on high above the signal lights of the

The Credo of Love

neighboring railway, she made him repeat again and again his wonderful verses:

Moi, je crois à l'amour comme je crois en Dieu.

And it was delightful!

Unfortunately, it did not last. The husband left them too much undisturbed. The fact is, *that man* was a philosopher. His wife gone, he had closed the green door of his oasis and quietly set about trimming his roses again, happy in the thought that these at least, attached to the soil by long roots, would not be able to run away from him. Our reassured lovers returned to Paris and then suddenly the young woman felt that some change had come over her poet. Their flight, fear of detection, and constant alarms, all these things which had fed her passion existed no longer, and she began to understand and see the situation clearly. Moreover, at every moment, in the settling of their little household, in the thousand paltry details of everyday life, the man she was living with showed himself more thoroughly.

The few and scarce generous, heroic or delicate feelings he possessed were spun out in his verses, and he kept

The Credo of Love

none for his personal use. He was mean, selfish, above all very niggardly, a fault love seldom forgives. Then he had cut off his moustaches, and was disfigured by the loss. How different from that fine gloomy fellow with his carefully curled locks, as he appeared one evening declaiming *Credo*, in the blaze of two chandeliers! Now, in the enforced retreat he was undergoing on her account, he gave way to all his crochets, the greatest of which was fancying himself as always ill. Indeed, from constantly playing at consumption, one ends by believing in it. The poet Amaury was fond of decoctions, wrapped himself up in plaisters, and covered his chimney piece with phials and powders. For some time the little woman took up quite seriously her part of a nursing sister. Her devotion seemed to excuse her fault and give an object to her life. But she soon tired of it. In spite of herself, in the stuffy room where the poet sat wrapped in flannel, she could not help thinking of her little garden so sweetly scented, and the kind nurseryman, seen from afar in the midst of his shrubs and flowerbeds, appeared to her as simple, touching, and disinterested as this other one was exacting and egotistical.

At the end of a month, she loved her husband, really loved him, not with the affection induced by habit, but with a real and true love. One day she wrote him a long

The Credo of Love

letter full of passion and repentance. He did not vouchsafe a reply. Perhaps he thought she was not yet sufficiently punished. Then she dispatched letter after letter, humbled herself, begged him to allow her to return, saying she would die rather than continue to live with "that man." Strange to say, she hid herself from him to write; for she believed him still in love, and while imploring her husband's forgiveness, she feared the exaltation of her lover.

"He will never allow me to leave," she said to herself. Accordingly, when by dint of supplications she obtained forgiveness and the nurseryman—I have already mentioned that he was a philosopher—consented to take her back, the return to her own home bore all the mysterious and dramatic aspect of flight. She literally eloped with her husband. It was her last culpable pleasure. One evening as the poet, tired of their dual existence, and proud of his regrown moustaches, had gone to an evening party to recite his *Credo of Love*, she jumped into a cab that was awaiting her at the end of the street and returned with her old husband to the little garden at Auteuil, forever cured of her ambition to be the wife of a poet. It is true that this fellow was not much of a poet!

THE TRANSTEVERINA

The play was just over and while the crowd, with its varied impressions, hurried away and poured out under the glare of the principal portico of the theatre, a few friends, of whom I was one, awaited the poet at the artists' entrance in order to congratulate him. His production had not, indeed, been very successful. Too powerful to suit the timid and trivial imagination of the public of our day, it was quite beyond the range of the stage, limited as that is by conventionalities and tolerated traditions. Pedantic criticism declared: "It is not fit for the stage!" and the scoffers of the boulevards revenged themselves for the emotion these magnificent verses had given them by repeating: "It won't pay!" As for us, we were proud of the friend who had dared to roll forth, in a ringing peal, his splendid golden rhymes, flashing the best product of his genius beneath the artificial and murderous light of the lustres, and presenting his characters life-sized, heedless of the optical illusion of the modern stage, of the dimness of opera-glass and defective vision.

The Transteverina

Amid a motley crowd of scene shifters, firemen, and *figurants* muffled up in comforters, the poet approached us, his tall figure bent double, his coat collar chillily turned up over his thin beard and long grizzled hair. He seemed depressed. The scant applause of the hired claque and literary friends confined to a corner of the house foretold a limited number of productions, choice and rare spectators, and posters rapidly replaced without giving his name a chance of being known. When one has worked twenty years, when one has reached the full maturity of talent and life, this obstinate refusal of the public to comprehend is wearying and disheartening, and one ends by thinking: "Perhaps after all they are right." Fear paralyses and words fail. Our acclamations and enthusiastic greetings somewhat cheered him. "Really do you think so? Is it well done? 'Tis true I have given all I knew." And his feverish hands anxiously clutched ours, his eyes full of tears sought a sincere and reassuring glance. It was the imploring anguish of the sick person, asking the doctor: "It is not true, I'm not going to die?" No! poet, you will not die. The operettas and fairy pieces that have had hundreds of productions and thousands of spectators will be long since forgotten, scattered to the winds with their last playbills, while your work will ever remain fresh and living.

The Transteverina

As we stood on the now deserted pavement, exhorting and cheering him, a loud contralto voice vulgarized by an Italian accent burst upon us.

"Hullo, artist! Enough *pouégie*. Let's go and eat the *estoufato!*" At the same moment a stout woman wrapped up in a hooded cape and a red tartan shawl linked her arm in that of our friend, in a manner so brutal and despotic that his countenance and attitude became at once embarrassed.

"My wife," he said, then turning towards her with a hesitating smile:

"Suppose we take them home and show them how you make an *estoufato?*"

Flattered in the conceit of her culinary accomplishments, the Italian graciously consented to receive us, and five or six of us started off for the heights of Montmartre where they dwelt, to share their stewed beef.

I confess I took a certain interest in the artist's home life. Since his marriage our friend had led a very secluded existence, almost always in the country; but what I knew of his life whetted my curiosity. Fifteen years before, when in all the freshness of a romantic imagination, he had met in the suburbs of Rome a magnificent creature with whom he immediately fell desperately in love. Maria

The Transteverina

Assunta, her father, and a brood of brothers and sisters in-
habited one of those little houses of the Transtevera with
walls uprising from the waters of the Tiber, and with an
old fishing boat rocking level with the door. One day he
caught sight of the handsome Italian girl, with bare feet
in the sand, red skirt tightly pleated around her, and un-
bleached linen sleeves tucked up to the shoulders, catch-
ing eels out of a large gleaming wet net. The silvery scales
glistening through the meshes full of water, the golden
river and scarlet petticoat, the beautiful black eyes deep
and pensive, which seemed darkened in their musing by
the surrounding sunlight struck the artist, perhaps even
rather trivially, like some coloured print on the title-page
of a song in a music-seller's window. It so chanced that
the girl was heart-whole, having till now bestowed her
affections on a big tom-cat, yellow and sly, also a great
fisher of eels, who bristled up all over when anyone approached his mistress.

Beasts and men, our lover managed to tame all these
folk, was married at Santa-Maria of the Transtevera and
brought back to France the beautiful Assunta and her
cato.

Ah! Poor fellow, he ought also to have brought away at

The Transteverina

the same time some of the sunlight of that country, a scrap of the blue sky, the eccentric costume and the bulrushes of the Tiber, and the large swing nets of the *Ponte Rotto*; in fact the frame with the picture. Then he would have been spared the cruel disenchantment he experienced when, having settled in a modest flat on the fourth storey, on the heights of Montmartre, he saw his handsome Transteverina decked out in a crinoline, a flounced dress, and a Parisian bonnet, which, constantly out of balance on the top of her heavy braids, assumed the most independent attitudes. Under the clear cold light of Parisian skies, the unfortunate man soon perceived that his wife was a fool, an irretrievable fool. Not a single idea even lurked in the velvety depths of those beautiful black eyes, lost in infinite contemplation. They glittered like an animal's in the calm of digestion, or in a chance gleam of light, nothing more. Withal the lady was common, vulgar, accustomed to govern by a slap all the little world of her native hut, and the least opposition threw her into uncontrollable rages.

Who would have guessed that the fine mouth, straitened by silence into the purest shape of an antique face, would suddenly open to let flow torrents of vulgar abuse? Without respect for herself or for him, out loud, in the

The Transteverina

street, at the theatre, she would pick a quarrel with him, and indulge in scenes of fearful jealousy. To crown all, devoid of any artistic feeling, she was completely ignorant of her husband's profession and language, of manners, in fact of everything. The little French she could be taught, only made her forget Italian, and the result was that she composed a kind of half-and-half jargon which had the most comical effect. In short this love story, begun like one of Lamartine's poems, was ending like a novel of Champfleury's. After having for a long time struggled to civilize this old woman, the poet saw he must abandon the task. Too honorable to leave her, probably still too much in love, he made up his mind to shut himself up, see no one, and work hard. The few intimate friends he admitted to his house, saw that they embarrassed him and ceased to come. Hence it was that for the last fifteen years he had been living boxed up in his household like in a leper's cell.

As I pondered over this wretched existence, I watched the strange couple walking before me. He, slender, tall and round-shouldered. She, squarely built, heavy, shaking her shawl by an impatient shrug of her shoulders, with a free gait like a man's. She was terribly cheerful, her speech was loud, and from time to time she turned round to see if we followed, familiarly shouting and calling by name those of us she happened to know, accentuating her words by much gesticulation as she would have hailed a fishing boat on the Tiber. When we reached their house, the *concierge*, furious at seeing so noisy a crew at such an unearthly hour, tried to prevent our entry. The Italian and he had a fearful row on the staircase. We were all dotted about on the winding stairs dimly lighted by the dying gas, ill at ease, uncomfortable, hardly knowing if we ought not to come down again.

"Come, quick, let us go up," said the poet in a low tone, and we followed him silently, while, leaning over the banisters that shook under her weight and anger, the Italian let fly a volley of abuse in which Roman imprecations alternated with the vocabulary of the back slums. What a return home for the poet who had just roused the admiration of artistic Paris, and still retained in his fevered eyes the dazzling intoxication of his first performance! What a humiliating recall to everyday life!

It was only by the fireside in his little sitting room that the icy chill caused by this silly adventure was dispelled, and we should soon have completely forgotten it, had

The Transteverina

it not been for the piercing voice and bursts of laughter
of the signora whom we heard in the kitchen telling her
maid how soundly she had berated the *choulato!* When
the table was laid and supper ready, she came and seated
herself amongst us, having taken off her shawl, bonnet
and veil, and I was able to examine her at my leisure.
She was no longer handsome. The square face, the broad
heavy jaw, the coarse hair turning grey, and above all the
vulgar expression of the mouth, contrasted singularly with
the eternal and meaningless reverie of the dreamy gaze.
Resting her elbows on the table, familiar and shapeless,
she joined in the conversation without for an instant los-
ing sight of her plate. Just over her head, proud amid
all the melancholy rubbish of the drawing-room, a large
portrait signed by an illustrious name, stood out of the
surrounding shade—it was Maria Assunta at twenty. The
purple costume, the milky white of the pleated wimple,
the bright gold of the overabundant imitation jewelry, set
off magnificently the brilliancy of a sunny complexion,
the velvety shades of the thick hair growing low on the
forehead, which seemed to be united by an almost imper-
ceptible down to the superb and straight line of the eyebrows. How could such an exuberance of life and beauty
have deteriorated and become such a mass of vulgarity?

The Transteverina

And curiously while the Transteverina talked, I interrogated her lovely eyes, so deep and soft on the canvas.

The excitement of the meal had put her in a good humour. To cheer up the poet, to whom his mingled failure and glory were doubly painful, she thumped him on the back, laughed with her mouth full, saying in her hideous jargon, that it was not worthwhile for such a trifle to fling oneself head downwards from the *campanile del Duomo*.

"Isn't it true, *il cato*?" she added turning to the old tomcat crippled by rheumatism, snoring in front of the fire. Then suddenly, in the middle of an interesting discussion, she screamed out to her husband in a voice senseless and brutal as the crack of a rifle:

"Hey! artist! *la lampo qui filo!*"

The poor fellow immediately interrupted his conversation to wind up the lamp, humble, submissive, anxious to avoid the scene he dreaded, and which in spite of all, he did not escape.

On returning from the theatre we had stopped at the *Maison d'Or* to get a bottle of choice wine to wash down the *estoufato*. All along the road Maria Assunta had piously carried it under her shawl, and on her arrival she had placed it on the table where she could cast tender hooks upon it, for Roman women are fond of good wine. Al-

The Transteverina

ready twice or three times mistrustful of her husband's absence of mind, and the length of his arms, she had said:

"Mind the *boteglia*—you're going to break it."

At last, as she went off to the kitchen to take up with her own hands the famous *estoufato*, she again called out to him:

"Whatever you do, don't break the *boteglia*."

Unluckily, the moment his wife had disappeared, the poet seized the opportunity to talk about art, theatres, success, so freely and with so much gusto and vivacity, that—crash! By a gesture more eloquent than the others, the wonderful bottle was was thrown down and fell to the ground in a thousand pieces. Never have I beheld such terror. He stopped short, and became deadly pale. At the same moment, Assunta's contralto was heard in the next room, and the Italian appeared on the threshold with flashing eyes, lips swollen with rage, red with the heat of the kitchen range.

"The *boteglia*!" she roared in a terrible voice.

Then timidly bending down to me, he whispered:

"Say it's you."

And the poor devil was so frightened, that I felt his long legs tremble under the table.

A COUPLE OF SINGERS

How could they help falling in love? Handsome and famous as they both were, singing in the same operas, living each night during five whole acts the same artificial and passionate existence. You cannot play with fire without being burnt. You cannot say twenty times a month: "I love you!" to the sighing of a flute or the tremolos of a violin, without at last being caught by the emotion of your own voice. In course of time, passion awoke in the surrounding harmonies, the rhythmical surprises, the gorgeousness of costume and scenery. It was wafted to them through the window that Elsa and Lohengrin threw wide open on a night vibrating with sound and luminousness:

"Come let us breathe the intoxicating perfumes."

It slipped in between the white columns of the Capulets' balcony, where Romeo and Juliet linger in the dawning light of day:

"It was the nightingale, and not the lark."

And softly it caught Faust and Marguerite in a ray of

A Couple of Singers

moonlight, that rose from the rustic bench to the shutters of their little chamber, amid the entangled ivy and blossoming roses:

"Let me once more gaze upon thy face."

Soon all Paris knew their love and became interested in it. It was the wonder of the season. The world came to admire the two splendid stars gently gravitating towards each other in the musical firmament of the Opera House. At last one summer evening, after an enthusiastic recall, as the curtain fell, separating the house full of noisy applause and the stage littered with bouquets, where the white gown of Juliet swept over scattered camellia blossoms, the two singers were seized with an irresistible impulse, as though their love, a shade artificial, had but awaited the emotion of a splendid success to reveal itself. Hands were clasped, vows exchanged, vows consecrated by the distant and persistent plaudits of the house. The two stars had made their conjunction.

After the wedding, some time passed before they were again seen on the stage. Then, when their holiday was ended, they reappeared in the same piece. This reappearance was a revelation. Until then, of the two singers, the man had been the most prized. Older and more accus-

A Couple of Singers

tomed to the public, whose foibles and preferences he had studied, he held the pit and boxes under the spell of his voice. Beside him, the other one seemed but an admirably gifted pupil, the promise of a future genius; but her voice was young and had angles in it, just as her shoulders were too slight and thin. And when on her return she appeared in one of her former parts, and the full rich, powerful sound poured out in the very first notes, abundant and pure, like the water of some sparkling spring, there ran through the house such a thrill of delight and surprise, that all the interest of the evening was concentrated on her. For the young woman, it was one of those happy days, in which the ambient atmosphere becomes limpid, light and vibrating, wafting towards one all the radiance and adulations of success. As for the husband, they almost forgot to applaud him, and as a dazzling light ever seems to make the shade around it darker, so he found himself relegated, as it were, to the most insignificant part of the stage, as if he were neither more nor less than a mere walking gentleman.

After all, the passion that was revealed in the song-stress's acting, in her voice full of charm and tenderness, was inspired by him. He alone lent fire to the glances of

A Couple of Singers

those deep eyes, and that idea ought to have made him proud, but the comedian's vanity proved stronger. At the end of the performance he send for the leader of the *claque* and berated him soundly. They had missed his entry and his exit, forgotten the recall at the third act; he would complain to the manager, &c.

Alas! In vain he struggled, in vain did the paid applause greet him; the good graces of the public, henceforth bestowed on his wife, remained definitively in her possession. She was fortunate too in a choice of parts appropriate to her talent and her beauty, in which she appeared with all the assurance of a woman of the world entering a ball-room, dressed in the colours best suited to her, and certain of an ovation. At each fresh success the husband was depressed, nervous, and irritable. The vogue which left him and so absolutely became hers only, seemed to him a kind of robbery. For a long while he strove to hide from everyone, more especially from his wife, this unavoidable anguish; but one evening, as she was going up the stairs leading to her dressing-room, holding up with both hands her skirt laden with bouquets, carried away by her triumphal success, she said to him with a voice still overcome by the excitement of applause: "We have had a

A Couple of Singers

magnificent house tonight." He replied: "You think so!" in such an ironical and bitter tone, that the young wife suddenly understood all.

Her husband was jealous! Not with the jealousy of a lover, who will only allow his wife to be beautiful for him, but with the jealousy of an artist, cold, furious, implacable. At times, when she stopped at the end of an air and multitudes of bravos were thrown to her from outstretched hands, he affected an indifferent and absent manner, and his listless gaze seemed to say to the spectators: "When you have finished applauding, I'll sing."

Ah! The applause, that sound like hail re-echoing through the lobbies, the house, and the side scenes, once the sweets of it are tasted, it is impossible to live without it. Great actors do not die of illness or old age, they cease to exist when applause no longer greets them. At the indifference of the public, this one was really seized with a feeling of despair. He grew thin, became peevish and bad-tempered. In vain did he reason with himself, look his incurable folly well in the face, repeat to himself before he came on the stage:

"And yet she is my wife, and I love her!"

In the artificial atmosphere of the stage the true senti-

A Couple of Singers

ment of life vanished at once. He still loved the wife, but detested the singer. She realized it, and as one nurses an invalid, watched the sad mania. At first she thought of lessening her success, of making a sparing use and not giving the full power of her voice and talent; but her resolutions like those of her husband could not withstand the glare of the footlights. Her talent, almost unconsciously, overstepped her will. Then she humbled herself before him, belittled herself. She asked his advice, inquired if he thought her interpretation correct, if he understood the part in that way.

Of course he was never satisfied. With assumed good-nature, in the tone of false friendship that performers use so much amongst each other, he would say, on the evenings of her greatest success:

"You must watch yourself, dear, you are not doing very well just now, not improving."

At other times he tried to prevent her singing:

"Take care, you are lavishing yourself. You are doing too much. Don't wear out your luck. Believe me, you ought to take a holiday."

He even condescended to the most paltry pretexts. Said she had a cold, was not in good voice. Or else he would try to pick some mean stage quarrel:

A Couple of Singers

"You took up the end of the duet too quickly; you spoilt my effect. You did it on purpose."

He never saw, poor wretch, that it was he who hindered her byplay, hurrying on with his cue in order to prevent any applause, and in his anxiety to regain the public ear, monopolizing the front of the stage, leaving his wife in the background. She never complained, for she loved him too well; moreover success makes us indulgent and every evening she was compelled to quit the shade in which she strove to conceal and efface herself, to obey the summons enthusiastically calling her to the footlights. The singular jealousy was soon noticed at the theatre, and their fellow actors made fun of it. They overwhelmed the singer with compliments about his wife's singing. They thrust under his eyes the newspaper article in which after four long columns devoted to the star, the critic bestowed a few lines to the fast-fading vogue of the husband. One day, having just read one of those articles, he rushed into his wife's dressing-room, holding the open paper in his hand and said to her, pale with rage:

"The fellow must have been your lover." He had indeed reached this degree of injustice. In fact the unhappy woman, praised and envied, whose name figured in large type on the playbills and might be read on all the walls

A Couple of Singers

of Paris, who was seized upon as a successful advertising medium and placed on the tiny gilt labels of the confectioner or perfumer, led the saddest and most humiliating of lives. She dared not open a paper for fear of reading her own praises, wept over the flowers that were thrown to her and which she left to die in a corner of her dressing-room, that she might avoid perpetuating at home the cruel memories of her triumphant evenings. She even wanted to quit the stage, but her husband objected.

"It will be said that I made you leave it."

And the horrible torture continued for both.

One evening at a premiere, the songstress was going onstage, when somebody said to her: "Mind what you are about. There is a cabal in the house against you." She laughed at the idea. A cabal against her? And for what reason, good heavens! She who only met with sympathy, who did not belong to any coterie! It was true however. In the middle of the opera, in a grand duet with her husband, at the moment when her magnificent voice had reached the highest pitch of its compass, finishing the sound in a succession of notes, even and pure like the rounded pearls of a necklace, a volley of hisses cut her short. The audience was as much moved and surprised as

A Couple of Singers

herself. All remained breathless, as though each one felt prisoner within them the passage she had not been able to finish. Suddenly a horrible, mad idea flashed across her mind. He was alone on the stage, in front of her. She gazed at him steadily and saw in his eyes the passing gleam of a cruel smile. The poor woman understood all. Sobs suffocated her. She could only burst into tears and blindly disappear through the crowded side scenes.

It was her own husband who had had her hissed!

A MISUNDERSTANDING

What can be the matter with him? What can he complain of? I cannot understand it. And yet I have done all I could to make him happy. To be sure, I don't say that instead of a poet I would not rather have married a notary or a lawyer, something rather more serious, rather less vague as a profession; nevertheless, such as he was he took my fancy. I thought him a trifle visionary, but charming all the same, and well-mannered; besides he had some fortune, and I thought that once married poetizing would not prevent him from seeking out some good appointments which would set us quite at ease. He too at that time seemed to find me to his taste. When he came to see me at my aunt's in the country, he could not find words enough to admire the order and arrangement of our little house, kept like a convent. "It is so quaint!" he used to say. He would laugh and call me all sorts of names taken from the poems and romances he had read. That shocked me a little I confess; I should have liked him to be more serious. But it was not until we were married and settled in Paris, that I felt all the difference of our two natures.

I had thought of everything, taken all my precautions. I would not have a Parisian, because Parisian women alarm me. I would not have a rich wife because she might be too exacting and extravagant. I also dreaded family ties, that terrible network of homely affections, which monopolizes, imprisons, dwarfs and stifles. My wife was the realization of my fondest dreams. I said to myself: "She will owe me everything." What pleasure to educate this simple mind to the contemplation of beauty, to initiate this pure soul to my enthusiasms and hopes, to give life, in short, to this statue! The fact is she had the air of a statue, with her great serious calm eyes, her regular Greek profile, her features, which although rather marked and severe, were softened by the rose-tinted bloom of youth and the shadow of the waving hair. Added to all this was a faint provincial accent that was my especial joy, an accent to which with closed eyes, I listened as a recollection of happy childhood, the echo of a tranquil life in some

A Misunderstanding

I had dreamed of a little home kept scrupulously bright and clean; instead of which, he began at once to encumber our apartment with useless old-fashioned furniture, covered with dust, and with faded tapestries, old as the hills. In everything it was the same. Would you believe that he obliged me to put away in the attic a sweetly pretty Empire clock, which had come to me from my aunt, and some splendidly framed pictures given me by my school friends. He thought them hideous. I am still wondering why? For after all, his study was one mass of lumber, of old smoky pictures; statuettes I blushed to look at, chipped antiques of all kinds, good for nothing; vases that would not hold water, odd cups, chandeliers covered with verdigris. By the side of my beautiful rosewood piano, he had put another, a little shabby thing with all the polish off, half the notes wanting, and so old and worn that one could hardly hear it. I began to think: "Good gracious! Is an artist then, really a little mad? Does he only care for useless things, and despise all that is useful?"

When I saw his friends, the society he received, it was still worse. Men with long hair, great beards, scarcely combed, badly dressed, who did not hesitate to smoke in my presence, while to listen to them made me quite uncomfortable, so widely opposed were their ideas to mine. They used long words, fine phrases, nothing natural, nothing simple. Then with all this, not a notion

A Misunderstanding

faraway, utterly unknown nook. And to think that now, this accent has become unbearable to me! But in those days, I had faith. I loved, I was happy, and disposed to be still more so. Full of ardour for my work, I had as soon as I was married begun a new poem, and in the evening I read to her the verses of the day. I wished to make her enter completely into my existence. The first time or two, she said to me: "Very pretty," and I was grateful to her for this childish approbation, hoping that in time she would comprehend better what was the very breath of my life.

Poor creature! How I must have bored her! After having read her my verses, I explained them to her, seeking in her beautiful astonished eyes the hoped-for gleam of light, ever fancying I should surprise it. I obliged to give her my opinion and I passed over all that was foolish to retain only what a chance inspiration might contain of good. I so longed to make of her my true helpmate, the real artist's wife! But no! She could not understand. In vain did I read to her the great poets, choosing the strongest, the tenderest—the golden rhymes of the love poems fell upon her ear as coldly and tediously as a hailstorm. Once I remember, we were reading *La Nuit d'Octobre*; she interrupted me, to ask for something more serious! I

A Misunderstanding

of ordinary civilities: you might ask them to dinner twenty times running, and there would be never a call, never a return of any kind. Not even a card or a bonbon on New Year's Day. Nothing. Some of these gentry were married and brought their wives to see us. You should have seen the style of these persons! For everyday wear, superb toilettes such as, thank heaven, I would wear at no time! And so ill-arranged, without order or method. Hair loose, skirts trailing, and such a bold display of their talents! There were some who sang like actresses, played the piano like professors, all talked on every subject just like men. I ask you, is this reasonable? Ought serious women once married to think of anything but the care of their household? This is what I tried to make my husband understand, when he was vexed at seeing me give up my music. Music is all very well when one is a little girl and has nothing better to do. But candidly, I should consider myself very ridiculous if I sat down every day to the piano.

Oh! I am quite aware that his great complaint against me is that I wished to draw him from the strange society I considered so dangerous for him. "You have driven away all my friends," he often used to say reproachfully. Yes, I did do so, and I don't regret it. Those creatures would have ended by driving him crazy. After leaving them, he would often spend the night in making rhymes and in marching up and down and talking aloud. As if

A Misunderstanding

tried to explain to her that there is nothing in the world more serious than poetry, which is the very essence of life, floating above it like a glory of light, in the vibrations of which words and thoughts are elevated and transfigured. Oh! what a disdainful smile passed over her pretty mouth and what condescension in her glance! As though a child or a madman had spoken to her.

What have I not thus wasted of strength and useless eloquence! Nothing was of any use. I stumbled perpetually against what she called good sense, reason, that eternal excuse of dried-up hearts and narrow minds. And it was not only poetry that bored her. Before our marriage, I had believed her to be a musician. She seemed to understand the pieces she played, aided by the underlinings of her teacher. Scarcely was she married when she closed her piano, and gave up her music. Can there be anything more melancholy than this abandonment by the young wife of all that had pleased in the young girl? The reply given, the part ended, the actress quits her costume. It was all done with a view to marriage; a surface of petty accomplishments, of pretty smiles, and fleeting elegance. With her the change was instantaneous. At first I hoped that the taste I could not give her, an artistic intelligence

A Misunderstanding

he were not already sufficiently eccentric and original in himself without being excited by others! What caprices, what whims, have I not put up with! Suddenly one morning, he would appear in my room: "Quick, get your hat—we are off to the country." Then one must leave everything, sewing, household affairs, take a carriage, go by rail, spend a mint of money! And I who only thought of economy! For after all, it is not with fifteen thousand francs (six hundred pounds) a year that one can be counted rich in Paris or make any provision for one's children. At first he used to laugh at my observations, and try to make me laugh; then when he saw how firmly I was resolved to remain serious, he found fault with my simplicity and my taste for home. Am I to blame because I detest theatres and concerts, and those artistic soirees to which he wished to drag me, and where he met his old acquaintances, a lot of scatterbrains, dissipated and Bohemian?

At one time, I thought he was becoming more reasonable. I had managed to withdraw him from his good-for-nothing circle of friends, and to gather round us a society of sensible people, well-settled into life, who might be of use to us. But no! Monsieur was bored. He was always bored, from morning till night. At our little soirees, where I was careful to arrange a whist table and a tea table, all as it should be, he would appear with such a face! With such a temper! When we were alone, it was just the

58

A Misunderstanding

and love of the beautiful, would come to her in spite of herself, through the medium of this wonderful Paris, with its unconscious refining influence on eyes and mind. But what can be done with a woman who does not know how to open a book, to look at a picture, who is always bored and refuses to sees anything? I soon understood that I must resign myself to have by my side nothing but a housewife, active and economical, indeed very economical. According to Proudhon, a woman, nothing more. I could have shaped my course accordingly; so many artists are in the same plight! But this modest role was not enough for her.

Little by little, slyly, silently, she managed to get rid of all my friends. We had not made any difference in our talk because of her presence. We talked as we always had done in the past, but she never understood the irony or the fantasy of our artistic exaggerations, of our wild axioms, or paradoxes, in which an idea is travestied only to figure more brilliantly. It only irritated and puzzled her. Seated in a quiet corner of the drawing-room, she listened and said nothing, planning all the while how she should eliminate one by one those who so much shocked her. Notwithstanding the seeming friendliness of the welcome,

A Misunderstanding

*same. Nevertheless, I was full of little attentions. I used to say
to him: "read me something of what you are doing." He recited
to me verses, tirades, of which I understood nothing, but I put
on an air of interest, and here and there made some little remark,
which, by the way, inevitably had the knack of annoying him.
In a year, working night and day, he could only make of all his
rhymes, one single volume which never sold. I said to him: "Ah!
You see," just in a reasoning spirit, to bring him to something
more comprehensible, more remunerative. He got into a frightful
rage, and afterwards sank into a state of gloomy depression which
made me very unhappy. My friends advised me as well as they
could: "you see, my dear, it is the ennui and bad temper of an
unoccupied man. If he worked a little more, he would not be so
gloomy."*

*Then I set to work, and all my belongings too, to seek him an
appointment. I moved heaven and earth, I made I don't know
how many visits to the wives of government officials, heads of de-
partments; I even penetrated into a minister's office. It was a surprise I reserved for him. I said to myself: "We shall see whether
he will be pleased this time." At length, the day when I received
his nomination in a lovely envelope with five big seals, I carried
it myself to his table, half wild with joy. It was provision for the
future, comfort, self-content, the tranquility of regular work. Do*

A Misunderstanding

there could already be felt in my rooms that thin current of cold air, which warns that the door is open and that it is time to leave.

My friends once gone, she replaced them by her own. I found myself surrounded by an absurd set of worthies, strangers to art, who hated poetry and scorned it because "it made no money." On purpose the names of fashionable writers who manufacture plays and novels by the dozen were cited before me, with the remark: "So and so makes a great deal of money!"

Make money! this is the all-important point for these creatures, and I had the pain of seeing my wife think with them. In this fatal atmosphere, her provincial habits, her mean and narrow views were made still more odious by an incredible stinginess. Fifteen thousand francs (six hundred pounds) a year! It seemed to me that with this income we could live without fear of the morrow. Not at all! She was always grumbling, talking of economy, reform, good investments. As she overpowered me with these dull details, I felt all desire and taste for work ebb away from me. Sometimes she came to my table and scornfully turned over the scattered half-written pages: "Only that!" she would say, counting the hours lost upon the insignificant

61

A Misunderstanding

you know what he did? He said: "He would never forgive me."
After which he tore the minister's letter into a thousand pieces,
and rushed out, banging the doors. Oh! these artists, poor un-
settled brains taking life all the wrong way! What could be done
with such a man? I should have liked to talk to him, reason with
him. In vain. Those were indeed right, who had said to me: "He
is a madman." Of what use moreover to talk to him? We do
not speak the same language. He would not understand me, any
more than I understand him. And now, here we must sit and
look at each other. I see hatred in his glance, and yet I have true
affection for him. It is very painful.

A Misunderstanding

little lines. Ah! if I had listened to her, my glorious title of poet, which it has taken me so many years to win, would be now dragged through the black mire of sensational literature. And when I think that to this selfsame woman I had at first opened my heart, confided all my dreams; and when I think that the contempt she now shows me because I do not make money dates from the first days of our marriage; I am indeed ashamed, both of myself and her.

I make no money! That explains everything, the reproach of her glance, her admiration for fruitful commonplaces, culminating in the steps she took but lately to obtain for me I don't know what post in a government office.

At this, however, I resisted. No defence remains to me but this, a force of inertia, which yields to no assault, to no persuasion. She may speak for hours, freeze me with her chilliest smile, my thought ever escapes her. And we have come to this! Married and condemned to live together, leagues of distance separate us; and we are both too weary, too utterly discouraged, to care to make one step that might draw us together. It is horrible!

ASSAULT WITH VIOLENCE

Mr. Petitbry, Chamber Counsel

TO MADAME NINA DE B., AT HER
AUNT'S HOUSE, IN MOULINS.

Madame, in accordance with the wishes of Madame your
aunt, I have looked into the matter in question. I have
noted down one by one all the different points and sub-
mitted your grievances to the most scrupulous investiga-
tion. Well, on my soul and conscience, I do not find the
fruit ripe enough, or to speak plainly, I do not consider
that you have sufficient grounds to justify your petition
for a judicial separation. Let us not forget that the French
law is a very forthright kind of thing, totally devoid of
delicate feeling for nice distinctions. It recognizes only
acts, serious, brutal acts, and unfortunately it is these acts
we lack. Most assuredly I have been deeply touched while
reading the account of your first year of your married
life, so very painful to you. You have paid dearly for the
glory of marrying a famous artist, one of those men in
whom fame and adulation develop monstrous egotism,

Assault with Violence

and who under penalty of shattering the frail and timid life that would attach itself to theirs, must live alone. Ah! madame, since the commencement of my career, how many wretched wives have I not beheld in the same cruel position as yourself! Artists who live only by and for the public, carry nothing home to their hearth but fatigue from glory, or the melancholy of their disappointments. An ill-regulated existence, without compass or rudder, subversive ideas contrary to all social conventionality, contempt of family life and its happiness, cerebral excitement sought for in the abuse of tobacco and strong drink, without mentioning anything else, this constitutes the terrible artistic element from which your dear Aunt is desirous of withdrawing you; but I must repeat, that while I fully comprehend her anxiety, nay her remorse even at having consented to such a marriage, I cannot see that matters have reach a point calculated to warrant petition.

I have, however, set down the outlines of a judicial memorandum, in which your principal grievances are grouped and skillfully brought into prominence. Here are the principal divisions of the work:

1. *Insulting conduct of Monsieur towards Madame's family.*— Refusal to receive our Aunt from Moulins, who brought

Assault with Violence

us up, and is tenderly attached to us.—Nicknames such as *Tata Bobosse*, Fairy Carabossa, and others, bestowed on that venerable old maid, whose back is slightly bent. —Jests and quips, drawings in pen and pencil of aforesaid and her infirmity.

2. *Unsociableness.*—Refusal to see Madame's friends, to make wedding calls, to send cards, to answer invitations, etc.

3. *Wanton extravagance.*—Money lent without acknowledgement to all kinds of Bohemians.—Open house and free quarters, turning the house into an inn.—constant subscriptions for statues, tombs, and productions of unfortunate fellow artists.—Starting an artistic and literary magazine!!!

4. *Insulting conduct to Madame.*—Having said out loud when alluding to us: "What a fool!"

5. *Cruelty and violence.*—Excessive brutality on the part of Monsieur.—Rage on the slightest pretext.—Breakage of china and furniture.—Scandalous rows, offensive expressions.

All this, as you see, dear Madame, constitutes a somewhat respectable amount of evidence, but it is not however sufficient. We lack assault with violence. Ah! if we

Assault with Violence

had only an assault with violence, a tiny little assault before witnesses, our case would be grand! But now that you have put a hundred and fifty miles between your husband and yourself we can scarcely hope for an incident of this kind. I say "hope" because in the present state of affairs, a brutal act on the part of this man would be the most fortunate thing that could befall you.

I remain, Madame, awaiting your commands, your devoted and obedient servant,

Petitbry

P.S.—Violence before witnesses, of course!

TO MONSIEUR PETITBRY, IN PARIS.

What, Sir! Have we come to such a pass as this! Is this what your laws have made of antique French chivalry! So then, when a misunderstanding is often sufficient to separate two hearts forever, your law courts require acts of violence to justify such a separation. Is it not scandalous, unjust, barbarous, outrageous? To think that in order to regain her freedom, my poor darling will be obliged

Assault with Violence

to run her neck into the halter, to abandon herself to all the fury of that monster, to excite it even. But no matter, our mind is made up. An assault with personal violence is necessary. Well! We will have it. No later than tomorrow, Nina will return to Paris. How will she be received? What will take place there? I canot think of it without a shudder. At this idea my hand trembles, my eyes become dimmed. Ah! Monsieur, Ah! Monsieur Petitbry. Ah!

Nina's Unhappy Aunt

Mr. Marestang, Attorney
At the Law Court of the Seine.

TO MONSIEUR HENRI B.,
LITERARY MAN IN PARIS.

Be calm, be calm, be calm! I forbid your going to Moulins or rushing off in pursuit of the fugitive. It is more judicious and safer to await her return in your own house, by your fireside. In point of fact, what has taken place? You refused to receive that ridiculous and ill-natured old maid; your wife has gone to join her. You should have expected as much. Family ties are very strong in the heart

Assault with Violence

of such an extremely youthful bride. You were in too great a hurry. Remember that this Aunt brought her up, that she has no other relations in the world. She has her husband, you will say. Ah! my dear fellow, between ourselves we may admit that husbands are not always amiable. I know one more especially who in spite of his good heart is so nervous, so violent! I am well aware that hard work and artistic preoccupations have a good deal to do with it. Be that as it may, the bird has been scared, and has flown back to its former cage. Don't be alarmed, it won't stay there long. Either I am very much mistaken or the Parisian of yesterday will soon weary of the antiquated surroundings, and ere long miss the vivacities of her poet. Above all don't stir.

Your old friend,

Marestang

TO MONSIEUR MARESTANG,

ATTORNEY IN PARIS.

At the same moment with your rational and friendly letter, I received a telegram from Moulins, announcing Nina's return. Ah! what a true prophet you were! She is

Assault with Violence

coming back this evening, all alone, just as she left me,
without the slightest advance on my part. The thing now
will be to arrange so easy and agreeable a life for her,
that she shall never again be tempted to leave me. I have
laid in a stock of tenderness and patience during her week's
absence. There is only one point on which I remain
inflexible: I will not again receive that horrible *Tata Bobosse*, that bluestocking of 1820, who gave me her niece
only in the hopes that my modest fame would serve to
heighten hers. Remember, my dear Marestang, that ever
since my marriage this wicked little old woman has always come between my wife and me, pushing her hump
into all our amusements at the theatres, the exhibitions,
in society, in the country, everywhere in fact. And you
wonder after that, at my having displayed a certain haste
in getting rid of her, and packing her off to her good town
of Moulins. Indeed my dear fellow, you have no idea of
all the harm those old maids, suspicious and ignorant of
life, are capable of doing in a young household. This one
had stuffed my wife's pretty little head full of false, old-
fashioned, preposterous ideas, trumpery sentimentality of
the time of Ipsiboe or young Florange: "*Ah ! if my lady
love saw me!*" For her, I was a *poate*, the *poate* one sees on

7 1

Assault with Violence

the frontispieces of Renduel or Ladvocat, crowned with laurels, a lyre on his hips, and his short velvet-collared cloak blown aside by a Parnassian gust of wind. That was the husband she had promised her niece, and you may fancy how terribly my poor Nina must have been disappointed. Nevertheless I admit that I was very bungling with the dear child. As you say, I wanted to go ahead too rapidly, I frightened her. It was my part gently to modify all that the rather narrowing and false education of the convent and the sentimental dreams of the Aunt had effected, leaving the provincial perfume time to evaporate. However all this can be repaired since she is returning. She is returning, my dear friend! This evening, I shall go and meet her at the station and we shall walk home arm in arm, reconciled and happy.

Henri de B.

NINA DE B. TO HER AUNT IN MOULINS.

He was waiting for me at the station and greeted me with a smile and open arms, as though I were returning from some ordinary journey. You can imagine that I put on my iciest appearance. Directly I reached home, I shut myself up in my room, where I dined alone, pleading

Assault with Violence

fatigue. After which, I locked myself in. He came to bid me good-night through the keyhole, and to my great surprise, went away on tiptoe without anger or importunity. This morning, I called on Monsieur Petitbry, who gave me detailed instructions as to the way I was to act, the hour, place, witnesses. Ah! my dear Aunt, if you knew how frightened I am as the hour draws near. His violence is so dreadful. Even when he is gentle like yesterday, his eyes have flashes of lightning. However, I will try and be courageous in thinking of you, my darling Aunt. Besides, as Monsieur Petitbry said to me, it is only a short painful moment to get over, and then we will both resume our former quiet life, so calm and happy.

Nina de B.

FROM THE SAME TO THE SAME.

Dear Aunt, I am writing to you from my bed, torn by the emotions of that terrible scene. Who could have supposed that things would take this turn? Nevertheless I had taken every precaution. I had warned Marthe and her sister, who were to come at one o'clock, and I had chosen for the great scene the moment when on leaving the table, the servants are clearing away in the dining-room next

Assault with Violence

to the study. From early morn my plans were laid; an hour of scales and exercises on the piano, the *Cloches du monastère*, the *Rêveries de Rosellen*, all the pieces he hates. This did not prevent his working away without betraying the slightest irritability. At breakfast, the same patience. A detestable breakfast, scraps, and the sweet dishes he loathes. And if you had seen my costume! A dress with a cape some five years out of date, a little black silk apron, and uncurled hair! In vain I sought for some signs of irritation, that well-known straight line that Monsieur hollows out between his eyebrows at the least annoyance. Well no! nothing! Really I might have thought they had changed my husband. He said to me in a calm and rather sad tone:

"Ah, you have done your hair in the old way."

I hardly answered, not wishing to hurry on matters before my witnesses had arrived, and then, strangely enough, I felt somewhat moved and upset beforehand by the scene I was trying to get up. At last, after a few still shorter replies on my part, he rose from the table and went into his own room. I followed him trembling. I heard my friends stationing themselves in the little drawing-room, and Pierre who came and went, arranging the glasses and silver. The decisive moment had arrived. He

Assault with Violence

must now be brought to the needful point of violence, and it seemed to me this would be easy, after all I had done since the morning to irritate him.

When I entered his study I must have been very pale. I felt myself in the lion's cage. The thought flashed across me: "Suppose he killed me!" He did not present a very terrible appearance, however, leaning back on his divan, a cigar in his mouth.

"Do I disturb you?" I asked in my most ironical voice.

He replied gently:

"No. You see. I am not working."

Myself, viciously:

"Ah! indeed you don't work then at all, now?"

He, still very mild:

"You are mistaken, my dear. On the contrary, I work a great deal. Only our craft is one in which a great deal of work can be done without having a tool in hand."

I:

"And what may you be doing at this moment? Ah yes, I know, your play in verse; always the same thing for the last two years. It is certainly lucky that your wife had a fortune! That allows you to idle at your ease."

I thought he would have sprung upon me at this. Not

Assault with Violence

a bit of it. He came up to me and took hold of my hands gently:

"Come, is it to be always the same thing? Are we to begin our life of warfare again? If so, why did you come back?"

I confess I felt rather moved by his sad and affectionate tone; but I thought of you, my poor Aunt, of your exile, of his harsh conduct towards us, and that gave me courage. I said to him the bitterest, most wounding things I could think of—I know not what—that I wished to heaven I had never married an artist; that at Moulins, everyone pitied me; that I found my friends married to magistrates, serious, influential men, in good positions, while he—if even he made money—But no, Monsieur would work for fame only! And what fame! At Moulins no one knew him; at Paris, his pieces were hissed. His books did not sell. And so on, and so on. My brain seemed to whirl round as all the malicious words came from me one after the other. He looked at me without replying, in chilly anger. Of course this coldness exasperated me more still. I was so much excited, that I no longer recognized my own voice, raised to an extraordinary pitch, and the last words I screamed at him—I can't remember what unjust and mad remark it was—seemed to buzz indistinctly in my

Assault with Violence

ears. For a moment, I thought Monsieur Petitbry's assault with violence was an accomplished fact. Pallid, with set teeth, Henri made two steps towards me:

"Madame!"

Then suddenly, his anger fell, his face became impassive again, and he looked at me with so scornful, insolent and calm a glance, that my patience came to an end. I raised my hand, and gave him the best box on the ear I ever gave in my life. At the noise, the door opened, and my witnesses appeared solemn and indignant.

"Monsieur! This is infamous!"

"Yes, isn't it?" said the poor fellow, showing his red cheek.

You can imagine my confusion. Happily, I took the line of fainting, and melting into torrents of tears, which relieved me greatly. At present, Henri is in my room. He watches by me, nurses me, and is really most kind. What can I do? What a checkmate! This will not prove very satisfactory to Monsieur Petitbry.

Nina de B.

BOHEMIA AT HOME

I hardly fancy it would be possible to find in the whole of Paris a more lively and peculiar house than that of the sculptor Simaise. Life there is one continual round of festivities. At whatever hour you drop in upon them, a sound of singing and laughter, or the jingle of a piano, guitar, or tamtam greets you. You can never enter the studio without finding a waltz going on, or a set of quadrilles, or a game of battledore and shuttlecock, or else it is cumbered with all the litter and preparations for a ball; shreds of tulle and ribbons lying scattered among the sculptor's chisels; artificial flowers hanging over the busts, and spangled skirts spreading over groups of moist clay.

The fact is that four big daughters of sixteen to twenty-five years of age, all very pretty indeed, take up a great deal of room; and when these young ladies whirl round with their hair streaming down their backs, with floating ribbons, long pins, and showy ornaments, it really seems as if instead of four there were eight, sixteen, thirty-two Misses Simaise, the one as dashing as the other, talking

Bohemia at Home

and laughing loudly, with hoydenish manner peculiar to artists' daughters, with the studio jests, the familiarity of students, and knowing also better than anyone how to dismiss a creditor or blow up a tradesman impertinent enough to present his bill at an inopportune moment.

These young damsels are the real mistresses of the house. From early dawn the father works, chisels, models unceasingly, for he has not settled income. At first he was ambitious and strove to do good work; some early successful exhibitions promised him future fame; but the necessity of providing for the support of his family, the clothing, feeding and future establishment of his children, threw him back into the ordinary work of the trade. As for Madame Simaise, she never attended to anything.

Very handsome when she married, very much admired in the artistic world into which her husband introduced her, at first satisfied with being only a pretty woman, later on she resigned herself to the part of a woman who had been pretty. A creole by birth, at least such was her pretension—although it was asserted that her parents had never left Courbevoie—she spent the days from morning to night in a hammock swung up in turn in all the different rooms of the house, fanning herself and taking siestas,

Bohemia at Home

full of contempt for the material details of everyday life. She had so often sat to her husband as model for Hebes and Dianas, that she fancied her only duty was to pass through life carrying some emblem of a goddess, such as a crescent on her head or a goblet in her hand. Indeed the disorder of the establishment was a sight in itself. The least thing necessitated a full hour's search.

"Have you seen my thimble? Marthe, Eva, Genevieve, Madeleine, who has seen my thimble?"

The drawers, in which books, powder, rouge, spangles, spoons and fans are tossed at haphazard, though crammed full, contain absolutely nothing useful; moreover they belong to a strange piece of furniture, curious, battered and incomplete. And how peculiar is the house itself! As they are constantly changing their residence, they never have time to settle anywhere, and this merry household seems to be perpetually awaiting the setting to rights indispensable after a ball. Only so many things are lacking, that it is not worthwhile settling, and as long as they can put on a bit of finery, display themselves out of doors, with something of a meteor flash, a semblance of style and appearance of luxury, honour is saved! Encampment does not in any way distress this migratory tribe. Through the

Bohemia at Home

half-opened doors, their poverty is betrayed by the four
bare walls of an unfurnished chamber, or the litter of an
overcrowded room. It is bohemianism in the domestic
circle, a life full of improvidence and surprises.

At the very moment when they sit down to table, they
suddenly perceive that everything is wanting, and that the
breakfast must be sent out for at once. In this manner
hours are spent rapidly, bustling and idling, and herein lies
a certain advantage. After a late breakfast, one does not
need to dine, but can sup at the ball, which fills up nearly
every evening. These ladies also give evening parties. Tea
is drunk out of all kinds of queer receptacles, goblets, old
tankards, ancient glasses, Japanese shells, the whole chipped
and cracked by the constant moves. The serene calm of
both mother and daughters in the midst of this poverty
is truly admirable. They have indeed other ideas running
though the brain than mere housekeeping details. One
has plaited her hair like a Swiss girl, another is curled like
any English baby, and Madame Simaise, from the top of
her hammock, lives in the beatitude of her former beauty.
As for father Simaise, he is always delighted. As long as he
hears the merry laugh of his daughters around him, he is
ready cheerfully to assume all the weight of this disorderly

Bohemia at Home

existence. To him are addressed in a coaxing manner such requests as: "Papa, I want a bonnet. Papa, I must have a dress." Sometimes the winter is severe. They are in such request, receive so many invitations. Pooh! The father has but to get up a couple of hours earlier. They will have a fire only in the studio, where all the family will gather. The girls will cut out and make their own dresses, while the hammock ropes wing slowly to and fro, and the father works on, perched upon his high stool.

Have you ever met these ladies in society? The moment they appear there is a commotion. It is long since the first two came out, but they are always so well adorned and so smart, that they are in great request as partners. They have as much as the younger sisters, almost as much as the mother in former days; moreover they carry off their tawdry jewelry and finery so well, and have such charming easy manners, with the giddy laugh of spoilt children, and such a Spanish way of flirting with a fan. Nevertheless they do not get married. No admirer has ever been able to get over the sight of that singular home. The wasteful and useless extravagance, the want of plates, the profusion of old tapestry in holes, of antique and ungilt lustres, the draughty doors, the constant visits of creditors, the slat-

Bohemia at Home

ternly appearance of the young ladies in slipshod slippers and dressing gowns, put to flight the best intentioned. In truth, it is not everyone who could resign himself to hang up the hammock of an idle woman in his home for the rest of his life.

I am very much afraid that the Misses Simaise will never marry. They had, however, a golden and unique opportunity during the Commune. The family had taken refuge in Normandy, in a small and very litigious town, full of lawyers, attorneys, and businessmen. No sooner had the father arrived, than he looked out for orders. His fame as a sculptor was of service to him, and as in the public square of the town there happened to be a statue of Cujas done by him. All the notabilities of the place wanted to have their busts done. The mother at once fastened up the hammock in a corner of the studio, and the young ladies organized a few parties. They at once met with great success. Here at least, poverty seemed but an accident due to exile; the disorder of the establishment was accounted for. The handsome girls laughed loudly to themselves at their destitution. They had started off without anything; and nothing could be had now Paris was closed. It lent to them an extra charm. It called to mind

Bohemia at Home

traveling gypsies, combing their beautiful hair in barns, and quenching their thirst in streams. The least poetical compared them in their minds to the exiles of Coblentz, those ladies of Marie-Antoinette's court who, obliged to fly in haste, without powder or hoops, or bedchamber women, were driven to all sorts of makeshifts, learning to wait upon themselves, and keeping up the frivolity of the French court, smiling so piquantly without beauty-spots.

Every evening a throng of dazzled lawyers crowded Simaise's studio. To the sounds of a hired piano, all this little world danced the polka, waltzed, schottisched—they still schottische in Normandy. "I shall end by marrying off one," thought old Simaise; and the fact is if one had gone off, all the others would have followed suit. Unluckily the first never went off, but it was a near touch. Amongst the numerous partners of these young ladies, in that corps de ballet of lawyers, attorneys and solicitors, the most rabid dancer was a widowed lawyer, who was extremely attentive to the eldest daughter. He was called by them "the first dancing attorney," in memory of Moliere's ballets, and certainly, considering the rate at which the fellow whirled round, Papa Simaise might well build the greatest hopes on him. But then businessmen do not dance like everybody else. This fellow, all the time he was waltzing, reflected silently: "The Simaise family is charming. Tra, la la, la la la, but it's useless their trying to hurry me on, la la la la la la. I shall not propose till the gates of Paris are re-opened. Tra la la, and I shall be able to make all necessary inquiries, la la la!" thus thought the first dancing attorney, and in fact, directly the blockade of Paris was raised, he got his information about the family, and the marriage did not come off.

Since then the poor little creatures have missed many other chances. However, this has in no way spoilt the happiness of the singular household. On the contrary, the more they live, the merrier they are. Last winter they changed quarters three times, were sold up once, and not-withstanding all this, gave two large fancy balls!

FRAGMENT OF A WOMAN'S

LETTER FOUND IN THE RUE

NOTRE-DAME-DES-CHAMPS

What it has cost me to marry an artist! Oh, my dear! If I had known! But young girls have singular ideas about so many things. Just imagine that at the Exhibition, when I read in the catalogue the addresses of faraway quiet streets at the further end of Paris, I pictured to myself peaceable, stay-at-home lives, devoted to work and the family circle, and I said to myself (feeling beforehand a certainty that I should be dreadfully jealous), "That is the sort of husband to suit me. He will always be with me. We shall spend our days together; he at his picture or sculpture, while I read or sew beside him, in the concentrated light of the studio." Poor dear innocent! I had not the faintest idea then what a studio really was, nor of the singular creatures one meets there. Never, in gazing at those statues of bold undressed goddesses had the idea

Fragment of a Woman's Letter

occurred to me that there were women daring enough to—and that even I myself... Otherwise, I can assure you I should never have married a sculptor. No, indeed, most decidedly not! I must own, they were all against this marriage at home; notwithstanding my husband's fortune, his already famous name, and the fine house he was having built for us two. It was I alone who would have it so. He was so elegant, so charming, so eager. I thought, however, he meddled a little too much about my dress, and the arrangement of my hair: "Do your hair like this; so," and he would amuse himself by placing a flower in the midst of my curls with far greater skill than any one of our milliners. So much experience in a man was alarming, wasn't it? I ought to have distrusted him. Well, you will see. Listen.

We returned from our honeymoon. While I was busy setting myself in my pretty and charmingly furnished rooms, that paradise you know so well, my husband, from the moment of his arrival, had set to work and spent the days at his studio, which was away from the house. When he returned in the evening, he would talk to me with feverish eagerness of his next subject for exhibition. The subject was "a Roman lady leaving the bath." He wanted

Fragment of a Woman's Letter

the marble to reproduce that faint shiver of the skin at the contact of air, the moisture of the delicate textures clinging to the shoulders, and all sorts of other fine things which I no longer remember. Between you and me, when he speaks to me of his sculpture, I do not always understand him very well. However, I used to say confidently: "It will be very pretty," and already I saw myself treading the finely sanded walks admiring my husband's work, a beautiful marble sculpture gleaming white against the green hangings; while behind me I heard whispered: "the wife of the sculptor."

At last one day, curious to see how our Roman lady was getting on, the idea occurred to me, to go and take him by surprise in his studio, which I had not yet visited. It was one of the first times I had gone out alone, and I had made myself very smart, I can tell you. When I arrived, I found the door of the little garden leading to the ground floor, wide open. So I walked straight in; and, conceive my indignation, when I beheld my husband in a white smock like a stone mason, with ruffled hair, hands grimed with clay, and in front of him, upright on a platform, a woman, my dear, a creature, almost undressed, and looking just as composed in this airy costume

Fragment of a Woman's Letter

as though it were perfectly natural. Her wretched clothes covered with mud, thick walking boots, and a round hat trimmed with a feather out of curl, were thrown beside her on a chair. All this I saw in an instant, for you may imagine how I fled. Etienne would have spoken to me —detained me; but with a gesture of horror at the clay-covered hands, I rushed off to mama, and reached her barely alive. You can imagine my appearance.

"Good heavens, dear child! What is the matter?"

I related to mama what I had seen, where this dreadful woman was, and in what costume. And I cried, and cried. My mother, much moved, tried to console me, explained to me that it must have been a model.

"What! But it is abominable; no one ever told me about that before I was married!"

Hereupon Etienne arrived, greatly distressed, and tried in his turn to make me understand that a model is not a woman like other women, and that besides sculptors cannot get on without them; but these reasons had no effect upon me, and I stoutly declared I would have nothing to do with a husband who spent his days tête-à-tête with young ladies in such a costume.

"Come, my dear Etienne," said poor mama, trying

Fragment of a Woman's Letter

hard to arrange everything peaceably, "could you not out of respect for your wife's feelings, replace this creature by a dummy, a lay figure?"

My husband bit his moustaches furiously.

"Quite impossible, dear mother."

"Still, my dear, it seems to me—a bright idea! Milliners have pasteboard heads on which they trim bonnets. Well, what can be done for a head, could it not be done for—?" It seems this is not possible. At least, this was what Etienne tried to demonstrate at great length, with all sorts of details and technical words. He really looked very unhappy. I watched him out of the corner of my eye while I dried my tears, and I saw that my grief affected him deeply. At last, after an endless discussion, it was agreed that since the model was indispensable, I should be there whenever she came. There chanced to be on one side of the studio a very convenient little lumber-room, from which I could see without being seen. I ought to be ashamed, you will say, of being jealous of such kind of creatures, and of showing my jealousy. But, my pet, you must have gone through these emotions before you can offer an opinion about them.

Next day, the model was to be there. I therefore sum-

Fragment of a Woman's Letter

moned up my courage, and installed myself in my hiding place, with the express condition that at the least tap at the partition my husband should come to me at once. Scarcely had I shut myself in, when the dreadful model I had seen the other day arrived, dressed Heaven knows how, and so wretched in appearance, that I asked myself how I could have been jealous of a woman who could walk abroad without a scrap of white cuff at her wrists, and in an old shawl with green fringe. Well, my dear, when I saw this creature throw off shawl and dress in the middle of the studio, and begin to undress in the coolest and boldest manner, it had an effect upon me I cannot describe. I choked with rage. I thumped at the partition. Etienne came to me. I trembled; I was pale. He laughed at me, gently reassured me, and returned to his work. By this time the woman was standing up, half-naked, her thick hair loosened and hanging down her back in glossy heaviness. It was no longer the poor wretch of a moment ago, but already almost a statue notwithstanding her common and listless air. My heart died within me. However, I said nothing. All at once, I hear my husband cry: "The left leg; the left leg forward." And as the model did not understand him at once, he went to her, and—Oh!

Fragment of a Woman's Letter

I could contain myself no longer. I knocked. He did not hear me. I knocked again, furiously. This time he ran to me, frowning a little at being disturbed in the heat of work. "Come, Armande, do be reasonable!" Bathed in tears, I leant my head upon his shoulder, and sobbed out: "I can't bear it, my dear, I can't; indeed, I can't!" At this, without answering me, he went sharply into the studio, and made a sign to that horror of a woman, who dressed herself and departed.

For several days, Etienne did not return to the studio. He remained at home with me, would not go out, refused even to see his friend; otherwise he was quite kind and gentle, but he had such a melancholy air. Once I asked him timidly: "you are not working any more?" which earned me this reply: "One can't work without a model." I had not the courage to pursue the subject, for I felt how much I was to blame, and that he had a right to be vexed with me. Nevertheless, by dint of caresses and endearments, I cajoled him into returning to his studio and trying to finish the statue—how do they say it?—out of his head, from imagination, in short, by mama's process. To me, this seemed quite feasible; but it gave the poor fellow endless trouble. Every evening he came in, with irritated

Fragment of a Woman's Letter

nerves and more and more discouraged; almost ill, indeed. To cheer him up, I used often to go and see him. I always said: "It is charming." But, as a fact, the statue made no progress whatever. I don't even know if he worked at it. When I arrived, I would find him always smoking on his divan, or perhaps, rolling up pellets of clay, which he angrily threw against the opposite wall.

One afternoon, when I was gazing at the unfortunate Roman lady, who, half modeled, had been so long in stepping out of her bath, an idea occurred to me. The Roman lady was about the same figure as myself; perhaps at a pinch I might....

"What do you mean by a well-turned leg?" I asked my husband suddenly.

He explained it to me at great length, showing me all that was still lacking to his statue, and which he could by no means give it without a model. Poor fellow! He had such a heartbroken air as he said this. Do you know what I did? Well, I bravely picked up the drapery which was lying in a corner, I went into my hiding place; then, very softly without saying a word, while he was still looking at his statue, I placed myself on the platform in front of him, in the costume and attitude in which I had seen

Fragment of a Woman's Letter

that abominable model. Ah my dear! What emotion I felt when he raised my eyes! I could have laughed and cried. I was blushing all over. And that tiresome muslin took so much arranging. Never mind! Etienne was so delighted that I was soon reassured. Indeed, to hear him, my dear, you might suppose—.

A GREAT MAN'S WIDOW

No one was astonished at hearing she was going to marry again. Notwithstanding all his genius, perhaps even on ac-count of his genius, the great man had for fifteen years led her a hard life, full of caprices and mad freaks that had attracted the attention of all Paris. On the high road to fame, over which he had so triumphantly and hurriedly traveled, like those who are to die young, she had sat behind him, humbly and timidly, in a corner of the chariot, ever fearful of collisions. Whenever she complained, relatives, friends, everyone was against her: "Respect his weaknesses," they would say to her, "they are the weaknesses of a god. Do not disturb him, do not worry him. Remember that your husband does not belong exclusively to you. He belongs much more to Art, to his country, than to his family. And who knows if each of the faults you reproach him with has not given us some sublime creation?" At last, however, her patience was worn out, she rebelled, became indignant and even unjust, so much indeed, that at the moment of the great

A Great Man's Widow

man's death, they were on the point of demanding a judicial separation and ready to see their great and celebrated name dragged into the columns of a society paper.

After the agitation of this unhappy match, the anxieties of the last illness, and the sudden death which for a moment revived her former affection, the first months of her widowhood acted on the young woman like a healthy calming water-cure. The enforced retirement, the quiet charm of mitigated sorrow, lent to her thirty-five years a second youth almost as attractive as the first. Moreover black suited her, and then she had the responsible and rather proud look of a woman left alone in life, with all the weight of a great name to carry honourably. Mindful of the fame of the departed one, that wretched fame that had cost her so many tears, and now grew day by day, like a magnificent flower nourished by the black earth of the tomb, she was to be seen draped in her long somber veils holding interviews with theatrical managers and publishers, busying herself in getting her husband's operas put again on the stage, superintending the printing of his posthumous works and unfinished manuscripts, bestowing on all these details a kind of solemn care and as it were the respect for a shrine.

A Great Man's Widow

It was this moment that her second husband met her. He too was a musician, almost unknown it is true, the author of a few waltzes and songs, and of two little operas, of which the scores, charmingly printed, were scarcely more played than sold. With a pleasant countenance, a handsome fortune that he owed to his exceedingly bourgeois family, he had above all an infinite respect for genius, a curiosity about famous men, and the ingenuous enthusiasm of a still youthful artist. Thus when he met the wife of the great man, he was dazzled and bewildered. It was as though the image of the glorious muse herself had appeared to him. He at once fell in love, and as the widow was beginning to receive a few friends, he had himself presented to her. There his passion grew in the atmosphere of genius that still lingered in all the corners of the drawing-room. There was the bust of the master, the piano he composed on, his scores spread over all the furniture, melodious even to look at, as though from between their half-opened pages, the written phrases re-echoed musically. The actual and very real charm of the widow surrounded by those austere memories as by a frame that became her, brought his love to a climax.

After hesitating a long time, the poor fellow at last pro-

A Great Man's Widow

posed, but in such humble and timid terms! "He knew how unworthy he was of her. He understood all the regret she would feel, in exchanging her illustrious name for his, so unknown and insignificant." And a thousand other artless phrases in the same style. In reality, the lady was indeed very much flattered by her conquest; however, she played the comedy of a broken heart, and assumed the disdainful, wearied airs of a woman whose life is ended without hopes of renewal. She, who had never in her life been so quiet and comfortable as since the death of her great man, she actually found tears with which to mourn for him, and an enthusiastic ardour in speaking of him. This, of course, only inflamed her youthful adorer the more and made him more eloquent and persuasive. In short, this severe widowhood ended in a marriage; but the widow did not abdicate, and remained—although married—more than ever the widow of a great man; well knowing that herein lay, in the eyes of her second husband, her real prestige. As she felt herself much older than he, to prevent his perceiving it, she overwhelmed him with her disdain, with a kind of vague pity, and unexpressed and offensive regret at her condescending marriage. However, he was not wounded by it, quite the contrary. He was

A Great Man's Widow

so convinced of his inferiority and thought it so natural that the memory of such a man should reign despotically in her heart! In order the better to maintain in him this humble attitude, she would at times read over with him the letters the great man had written to her when he was courting her. This return towards the past rejuvenated her some fifteen years, lent her the assurance of a handsome and beloved woman, seen through all the wild love and delightful exaggeration of written passion. That she had since then changed, her young husband cared little, loving her on the faith of another, and drawing therefrom I know not what strange kind of vanity. It seemed to him that these passionate appeals added to his own, and that he inherited a whole past of love.

A strange couple indeed! It was in society, however, that they presented the most curious spectacle. I sometimes caught sight of them at the theatre. No one would have recognized the timid and shy young woman, who formerly accompanied the maestro, lost in the gigantic shadow he cast around him. Now, seated upright in the front of the box, she displayed herself, attracting all eyes by the pride of her own glance. It might be said that her head was surrounded by her first husband's halo of glory,

A Great Man's Widow

his name re-echoing around her like a homage or a reproach. The other one, seated a little behind her, with the
subservient physiognomy of one ready for every abnegation in life, watched each of her movements, ready to
attend to her slightest wish.

At home, the peculiarity of their attitude was still more
noticeable. I remember a certain evening party they gave
a year after their marriage. The husband moved about
among the crowd of guests, proud but rather embarrassed at gathering together so many in his own house.
The wife, disdainful, melancholy, and very superior, was
on that evening more than ever the widow of a great
man! She had a peculiar way of glancing at her husband
from over her shoulder, of calling him "my poor dear
friend," of casting on him all the wearisome drudgery
of the reception, with an air saying: "You are only fit
for that." Around her gathered a circle of former friends,
those who had been spectators of the brilliant debuts of
the great man, of his struggles, and his success. She sim-
pered to them; played the young girl! They had known
her so young! Nearly all of them called her by her Chris-
tian name, "Anais." They formed a kind of coenaculum,
which the poor husband respectfully approached, to hear
his predecessor spoken of. They recalled the glorious *first*

A Great Man's Widow

nights, those evenings on which nearly every battle was won, and the great man's manias, his way of working; how, in order to summon up inspiration, he insisted on his wife being at his side, decked out in full ball dress. "Do you remember, Anais?" And Anais sighed and blushed.

It was at that time that he had written his most tender pieces, above all *Savonarole*, the most passionate of his creations, with a grand duet, interwoven with rays of moonshine, the perfume of roses and the warbling of nightingales. An enthusiast sat down and played it on the piano, amid a silence of attentive emotion. At the last note of the magnificent piece, the lady burst into tears. "I cannot help it," she said, "I have never been able to hear it without weeping." The great man's old friends surrounded his unhappy widow with sympathetic expressions, coming up to her one by one, like at a funereal ceremony, to give a thrilling clasp to her hand.

"Come, come, Anais, be courageous."

And the drollest thing was to see the second husband, standing by the side of his wife, deeply touched and affected, shaking hands all round, and accepting, he too, his share of sympathy. "What genius! What genius!" he repeated as he mopped his eyes. It was at the same time ridiculous and affecting.

THE DECEIVER

I have loved but one woman in my life, the painter D—— said one day to us. I spent five years of perfect happiness and peaceful, fruitful tranquility with her. I may say that to her I owe my present celebrity, so easy was work, and so spontaneous was inspiration by her side. Even when I first met her, she seemed to have been mine from time immemorial. Her beauty, her character were the realization of all my dreams. That woman never left me; she died in my house, in my arms, loving to the last. Well, when I think of her, it is with a feeling of rage. If I strive to recall her, the same as I ever saw her during those five years, in all the radiance of love, with her lither yielding figure, the gilded pallor of her cheeks, her Oriental Jewish features, regular and delicate in the soft roundness of her face, her slow speech as velvety as her glance, if I seek to embody that charming vision, it is only in order the more fiercely to cry to it: "I hate you!"

Her name was Clotilde. At the house of the mutual acquaintances where we met, she was known under the

The Deceiver

name of Madame Deloche, and was said to be the widow of a captain of the merchant service. Indeed, she appeared to have traveled a great deal. In the course of conversation, she would suddenly say: When I was at Tampico; or else: once in the harbour at Valparaiso. But apart from this, there was no trace in her manners or language of a wandering existence, nothing betrayed disorder or precipitation of sudden departures or abrupt returns. She was a thorough Parisian, dressed in perfect good taste, without any of those burnooses or eccentric *sarapes* by which one recognizes the wives of officers and sailors who are always arrayed in traveling costume.

When I found that I loved her, my first, my only idea was to ask her in marriage. Someone spoke on my behalf. She simply replied that she would never marry again. Henceforth I avoided meeting her; and as my thoughts were too wholly absorbed and occupied by her to allow me to work, I determined to travel. I was busily engaged in preparations for my departure, when one morning, in my own apartment, in the midst of all the litter of opened drawers and scattered trunks, to my great surprise, I saw Madame Deloche enter.

"Why are you leaving?" she said softly. "Because you love me? I also love. I love you. Only (and here her voice

The Deceiver

shook a little) only, I am married." And she told me her history.

It was a romance of love and desertion. Her husband drank, struck her! At the end of three years they had separated. Her family, of whom she seemed very proud, held a high position in Paris, but ever since her marriage they had refused to receive her. She was the niece of the Chief Rabbi. Her sister, the widow of a superior officer, had married for the second time a Chief Ranger of the woods and forests of Saint-Germain. As for her, ruined by her husband, she had fortunately had a very thorough education and possessed some accomplishments, by which she was able to augment her resources. She gave music lessons in various rich houses of the Chaussee d'Antin and Faubourg Saint Honore, and gained an ample livelihood.

The story was touching, although somewhat lengthy, full of the pretty repetitions, the interminable incidents that entangle feminine discourse. Indeed she took several days to relate it. I had hired for us two, a little house in the Avenue de l'Imperatrice, standing between the silent streets and peaceful lawns. I could have spent a year listening to and looking at her, without a thought for my work. She was the first to send me back to my studio, and I could not prevent her from again taking up her les-

The Deceiver

sons. I was touched by her concern for the dignity of her life. I admired the proud spirit, notwithstanding that I could not help being rather humiliated at her expressed determination to owe nothing save to her own exertions. We were therefore separated all day long, and only met in the evening in our little house.

With what joy did I not return home, what impatience I felt when she was late, and how happy I was when I found her there before me! She would bring me back bouquets and choice flowers from her journeys to Paris. Often I pressed upon her some present, but she laughingly said she was richer than I; and in truth her lessons must have been very well paid, for she always dressed in an expensively elegant manner, and the black dresses which, with coquettish care for her complexion and style of beauty she preferred, had the dull softness of velvet, the brilliancy of satin and jet, a confusion of silken lace, which revealed to the astonished eye, under an apparent simplicity, a world of feminine elegance in the thousand shades contained in a single colour.

Moreover her occupation was by no means laborious, she said. All her pupils, daughters of bankers or stock brokers, loved and respected her; and many a time she would show me a bracelet or a ring that had been presented as a

The Deceiver

mark of gratitude for her care. Except for our work, we never left one another, and we went nowhere. Only on Sundays she went off to Saint-Germain to see her sister, the wife of the Chief Ranger, with whom she was now reconciled. I would accompany her to the station. She would return the same evening, and often in the long summer days, we would agree to meet at some station on the way, by the riverside or in the woods. She would tell me about her visit, the children's good looks, the air of happiness that reigned in the household. My heart bled for her, deprived of the pleasures of family life as she was doomed to be; and my tenderness increased tenfold in order to make her forget the falseness of her position, so painful to a woman of her character.

What a happy time of perfect coincidence, and how well I worked! I suspected nothing. All she said seemed so true, so natural. I could only reproach her with one thing. When talking of the houses she frequented, and the different families of her pupils, she would indulge in a superabundance of imaginary details and fancied intrigues, which she invented without any apropos. Calm herself, she was ever conjuring up romances around her, and her life was spent in composing dramatic situations. These idle fancies disturbed my happiness. I, who longed to leave

The Deceiver

the world and society, in order to devote myself exclusively to her, found her too much taken up by indifferent subjects. However, I could easily excuse this defect in a young and unhappy woman, whose life had been hitherto a sad romance, the issue of which could not be foreseen.

Once only did a suspicion or rather a presentiment cross my mind. One Sunday evening she failed to return home. I was in despair. What could I do? Go to Saint-Germain? I might compromise her. Nevertheless, after a dreadful night of anguish, I had decided on starting, when she arrived, looking pale and worried. Her sister was ill, she had been obliged to stay and nurse her. I believed all she told me, not distrusting the overflow of words called forth by the slightest question, which swamped the principal matter in a deluge of idle details: such as the hour of arrival, the rudeness of a guard, the lateness of the train. Twice or three times in the same week, she returned to Saint-Germain and slept there; then, her sister's illness over, she resumed her regular and peaceful existence.

Unfortunately, shortly after this, she in her turn fell ill. She came back one day from her lessons, shivering, wet, and fevered. Inflammation of the lungs set in; from the first her case was serious, and soon—the doctor told me— hopeless. My despair was maddening. Then I thought

The Deceiver

only of soothing her last moments. The family she loved so well, of which she was so proud, I would bring to her deathbed. Without letting her know, I first wrote to her sister at Saint-Germain, and I went off at once myself to her uncle, the Chief Rabbi. I hardly remember at what unreasonable hour I reached the house. Great catastrophes throw such a confusion into life and upset every detail. I fancy the good Rabbi was dining. He came out into the hall, wondering and amazed, to speak to me.

"Monsieur," I said to him, "there are moments when all hatred must cease."

He turned his venerable face towards me with a bewildered look.

I resumed:

"Your niece is dying!"

"My niece! But I have no niece; you are mistaken."

"Oh, Sir! I implore you, lay aside all foolish family rancour. I am speaking of Madame Deloche, the wife of Captain——"

"I do not know Madame Deloche. You are mistaken, my son, I assure you."

And he gently pushed me toward the door, taking me for a hoaxer or a madman. I must in fact have appeared very odd. What I heard was so unexpected, so terrible.

The Deceiver

She had lied to me then. Wherefore? Suddenly an idea flashed across me. I directed the cabman to drive me to the address of one of those pupils of whom she had so often spoken to me, the daughter of a well-known banker.

I inquired of the servant: "Madame Deloche?"

"There is no one here of that name."

"Yes, I know that. It is a lady who gives music lessons to your young ladies."

"We have no young ladies here, not even a piano. I don't know what you mean."

I made no further inquiries. I felt sure of meeting with the same answer, the same disappointment. On my return to our little house, they gave me a letter with the postmark of Saint-Germain. I opened it, instinctively guessing the contents. The Chief Ranger also had no knowledge of Madame Deloche. Moreover he had neither wife nor child.

This was the last blow. Thus for five years each of her words had been a lie. A thousand jealous thoughts took possession of me, and madly, hardly knowing what I was about, I entered the room in which she was dying. All the questions that were torturing me burst forth over that bed of suffering: "Why did you go to Saint-Germain on Sun-

The Deceiver

days? Where did you spend your days? Where did you spend that night? Come, answer me." And I bent over her, seeking in the depths of her still proud and beautiful eyes answers that I awaited with anguish; but she remained mute and impassive.

I resumed, trembling with rage: "You never gave any lessons. I have been everywhere. Nobody knows you. Whence came that money, those laces, those jewels?" She threw me a glance full of despairing sadness, and that was all. In truth, I ought to have spared her, and allowed her to die in peace. But I had loved her too well. My jealousy was stronger than my pity. I continued: "For five years you have deceived me, lying to me every day, every hour. You knew my whole life, and I knew nothing of yours. Nothing, not even your name. For it is not yours, is it, the name you bear? Ah liar! liar! What, she is going to die, and I do not even know by what name to call her! Come, tell me who you are? Whence come you? Why did you intrude into my life? Speak! Tell me something!"

Vain efforts! Instead of answering, she with difficulty turned her face to the wall, as though she feared that her last glance might betray her secret. And thus the unhappy creature died! Died without a word, liar to the last.

THE COMTESSE IRMA

"M. Charles d'Athis, literary man, has the honour to inform you of the birth of his son Robert.

"The child is doing well."

Some dozen years ago, all literary and artistic Paris received this little note on the glossiest of paper, embossed with the arms of the Counts of d'Athis-Mons, of whom the last Charles d'Athis had—while still young—succeeded in making for himself a genuine reputation as a poet.

"The child is doing well."

And the mother? Of her there was no mention in the note. Everyone knew her but too well. She was the daughter of an old poacher of Seine et Oise; a quondam model, named Irma Salle, whose portrait had figured in every exhibition, as the original had in every studio. Her low forehead, lip curled like an antique, this chance return of the peasant's face to primitive lines—a turkey keeper with Greek features—the slightly tanned skin common to

The Comtesse Irma

all whose childhood is spent in the open air, giving to fair hair reflections of pale silkiness, adorned this minx with a kind of wild originality, completed by a pair of magnificently green eyes, burning beneath heavy eyebrows.

One night, on leaving a *bal de l'Opera*, d'Athis had taken her to sup with him, and though this was two years ago, the supper still continued. But, whereas Irma had become completely a part of the poet's life, this intimation of the child's birth, curt and haughty as it was, sufficiently indicated how little she was considered by him. And in truth, in this temporary household, the woman was scarcely more than a housekeeper, showing in the management of the gentleman-poet's house the hard shrewdness of her dual nature of peasant and courtesan; and endeavouring, at no matter what price, to render herself indispensable. Too rustic, and too stupid to understand anything of d'Athis' genius, of those fine verses, fashionable and refined, which made him a sort of Parisian Tennyson, she nevertheless understood how to bend to all his whims, and be silent under his contempt; as if in the depths of that peasant nature lurked something of the boor's humble admiration for his lord. The birth of the child only served to accentuate her importance in the house.

The Comtesse Irma

When the dowager Comtesse d'Athis-Mons, the mother of the poet, a distinguished and very great lady, learned that a grandson was born to her, a sweet little Vicomte, duly recognized and authenticated by the author of his being,[*] she was seized with a wish to see and kiss the child. It was, to be sure, a rather bitter reflection for the former reader to Queen Marie-Amelie to think that the heir of such a great name should have such a mother; but, keeping strictly to the terms of the *billets de faire part* the venerable lady could forget that the creature existed. When she went to see the child out at nurse, she chose the days on which she would be sure to meet no one; she admired him, spoilt him, took him to heart, worshipped him with that grandmotherly adoration which is the last trove of a woman's life, giving her an excuse for living a few years longer in order to see the little ones spring up and growing around her. Then when the baby Vicomte was a little bigger and returned to live with his father and mother, a treaty was made, for the Comtesse could not give up her beloved visits; at the sound of the grandmoth-

---

[*] According to French law, an unmarried man recognizing his illegitimate child thereby confers on him all the rights of a legitimate one, including both title and fortune.

The Comtesse Irma

er's ring, Irma humbly and silently disappeared, or else the child was taken to his grandmother's house, and thus spoilt by his two mothers. He loved them equally, somewhat astonished to feel in the warmth of their caresses a kind of exclusiveness, a wish to monopolize. D'Athis, careless of everything but his verses, absorbed by his growing fame, was content to adore his little Robert, to talk of him to everyone and to imagine that the child belonged to him, and him only. This illusion did not last.

"I should like to see you married," his mother said to him one day.

"Yes, but how about the child?"

"Don't worry yourself about that. I have picked out for you a young girl of good family but poor, who adores you. I have introduced Robert to her, and they are already great friends. Besides, the first year I will keep the darling with me. Afterwards, we shall see."

"And—the mother?" hesitated the poet, reddening a little, for it was the first time that he had spoken of Irma to his mother.

"Pooh!" replied the old dowager, laughing, "we will settle something handsome on her, and I am quite sure

The Comtesse Irma

she will soon be married also. The bourgeois of Paris it not particular."

That very evening, d'Athis, who had never been desperately in love with his mistress, spoke to her of these arrangements and found her as usual—submissive and apparently docile to his will. But the next day, when he returned home, he found that mother and child had flown. Finally, they were discovered in a wretched hut on the border of the Forest of Rambouillet, with Irma's father; and when the poet arrived he found his son, his young prince, in his velvet and lace, jumping on the old poacher's knee, playing with his pipe, running after the hens, delighted to shake his fair curls in the fresh air. D'Athis, though much upset by emotion, pretended to laugh the affair off, and wished at once to take his fugitives home with him. But Irma did not see the matter in the same light. She had been dismissed; she took her child with her. What more natural? Nothing short of the poet's promise that he would give up all thoughts of marriage decided her to return. Moreover, she made her own conditions. It had been too long forgotten that she was Robert's mother. Always to disappear and hide whenever Madame d'Athis

The Comtesse Irma

appeared was no longer possible for her. The child was growing too old for her to be exposed to such humiliations before him. It was therefore agreed that as Madame d'Athis had refused to be brought into contact with her son's mistress, she should no longer go to his house, but that the child should be brought to her every day.

Then began for the old grandmother a regular torture. Every day fresh pretexts were made to keep the child away; he had coughed, it was too cold, it was raining. Then came his walks, rides, gymnastic exercises. The poor old lady never saw her grandson. At first she tried complaining to d'Athis; but women alone have the secret of carrying on these little warfares. Their ruses remain invisible, like the hidden stitches which catch back the folds and laces of their dress. The poet could see nothing of it; and the saddened grandmother spent her life in waiting for her darling's visit, in watching for him in the street, when he walked out with a servant; and these furtive kisses and hasty glances only augmented her maternal passion without satisfying it.

During this time, Irma Salle—always by means of the child—succeeded in gaining ground in the father's heart.

The Comtesse Irma

She was the recognized head of the house now, received visitors, gave parties, settled herself as a woman who means to remain where she is. Still she took care to say from time to time to the little Vicomte, before his father: "Do you remember the chickens at Grandpapa Salle's? Shall we go back and see them?" And by this everlasting threat of departure, she paved the way to the end she had in view—marriage.

It took her five years to become a Comtesse, but at length she gained her point. One day, the poet came in fear and trembling to announce to his mother that he had decided to marry his mistress, and the old lady, instead of being indignant hailed the calamity as a deliverance, seeing but one thing in the marriage; the possibility of once more entering her son's door, and of freely indulging her affection for her little Robert.

In truth, the real honeymoon was for the grandmother. D'Athis, after this rash act, wished to be away from Paris for a time. He felt uneasy there. And as the child, clinging to his mother's skirts, ruled the house, they all established themselves in Irma's native country, within hail of old father Salle's chickens. It was indeed the most curious,

The Comtesse Irma

the most ill-assorted household that could be imagined. Grandma d'Athis and Grandpapa Salle met each night at the evening toilet of their grandson. The old poacher, his short black pipe wedged into the corner of his mouth; and the former reader at the Tuileries, with her silvery hair, and her imposing manner, together watched the lovely child rolling before them on the carpet, and admired him equally. The one brought him from Paris the newest, most expensive, most showy toys; the other manufactured for him the most splendid whistles from bits of elder; and, by Jove! the Dauphin hesitated between them!

Upon the whole, among all these beings grouped as it were by force around a cradle, the only really unhappy one was Charles d'Athis. His elegant and patrician inspiration suffered from this life in the depths of a forest, like a delicate Parisian woman for whom the country air is too strong. He could no longer work, and far from that terrible Paris who shuts her gates so quickly against the absent, he felt himself already nearly forgotten. Fortunately the child was there, and when the child smiled, the father thought no more of his successes as a poet, nor of the past of Irma Salle.

And now, would you know the finale of the singular

The Comtesse Irma

drama? Read the brief note bordered with black, that I received only a few days ago, and which is the last page of this truly Parisian adventure:

"M. le Comte and Mme. La comtesse d'Athis grieve to inform you of the death of their son Robert."

Unhappy creatures! Imagine them all four gazing at each other before that empty cradle!

THE CONFIDENCES OF

AN ACADEMIC COAT

That morning was the dawn of a glorious day for the sculptor Guillardin.

Elected on the previous day a member of the *Institut*, he was about to inaugurate before the five Academies gathered together in solemn concourse, his academic coat, a magnificent garment ornamented with green palm leaves, resplendent in its new cloth and silken embroidery, colour of hope. The blessed coat, opened ready to slip on, lay spread on an armchair, and Guillardin contemplated it tenderly as he arranged the bow of his white tie.

"Above all no hurry," thought the good fellow. "I have plenty of time."

The fact is that in his feverish impatience he had dressed a couple of hours too soon; and the beautiful Madame Guillardin—always very slow over her dressing—had positively declared that on this day she would only be ready at the precise moment—not a minute earlier, do you hear!

The Confidences of an Academic Coat

Unfortunate Guillardin! What could he do to kill the time?

"Well, all the same, I will try on my coat," he said, and gently as though he were handing tulle and lace, he lifted the precious frippery, and having donned it with infinite precaution, he placed himself in front of his looking-glass. Oh! what a charming picture the mirror disclosed to him! What an amiable little Academician, freshly hatched, happy, smiling, grizzled, and protuberant, with arms too short in proportion to his figure, which in the new sleeves acquired a stiff and automatic dignity! Thoroughly satisfied with his appearance, Guillardin marched up and down, bowed as though entering the Academy, smiled to his colleagues of the fine arts, and assumed academical attitudes. Nevertheless, whatever pride one my feel at one's personal appearance, it is impossible to remain two hours in full dress, before a looking-glass. At last our Academician felt somewhat fatigued, and fearful lest he should rumple his coat, made up his mind to take it off and lay it back very carefully on the armchair. Then seating himself opposite on the other side of the fireplace, with his legs stretched out and his two hands crossed over his dress waistcoat, he began to indulge in sweet dreams as he gazed at the green coat.

The Confidences of an Academic Coat

Like the traveler who, arrived at the end of his journey, likes to remember the dangers and difficulties that have beset his path, Guillardin retraced his life, year by year, from the day when he began to learn modeling in Jouffroy's studio. Ah! the outset is hard in the confounded profession. He remembered the fireless winters, the sleepless nights, the endless walks in search of work, the desperate rage experienced at feeling so small, so lost, and unknown in the immense crowd that pushes, hustles, upsets, and rushes. And yet all alone, without patronage or money, he had managed to rise. By sheer talent, sir! And his head thrown back, and eyes half-shut, the worthy man kept repeating out loud to himself: "By sheer talent. Nothing but talent."

A long burst of laughter, dry and creaky like an old man's laugh, suddenly interrupted him. Slightly startled, Guillardin glanced around the room. He was alone, quite alone, tete-a-tete with his green coat, the ghost of an Academician solemnly spread out opposite him, on the other side of the fire. And still the insolent laugh rang on. Then as he looked at it more intently, the sculptor almost fancied that his coat was no longer in the place where he had put it, but really seated in the armchair, with tails turned up, and sleeves resting on the arms of the chair, the fronts

The Confidences of an Academic Coat

puffed out with an appearance of life. Incredible as it may seem, it was this thing that was laughing. Yes, it was from the singular green coat that arose the uncontrollable fits of laughter by which it was agitated, shaken and convulsed, causing it to jerk its tails, throw itself back in the chair, and at moments place its two sleeves against its sides, as though to check this supernatural and inextinguishable excess of mirth. At the same time, a feeble voice, sly and mischievous, could be heard saying between two hiccups: "Oh dear, oh dear, how it hurts one to laugh like this! How it hurts one to laugh like this!"

"Who the devil is there, for mercy's sake?" asked the poor Academician with wide staring eyes.

The voice continued still more slyly and mischievously:

"But it's I, Monsieur Guillardin, I, your palm-embroidered coat, waiting for you to start for the reception. I must crave pardon for having so unreasonably interrupted your musing; but really it is too funny to hear you talk of your talent! I could not restrain myself. Come, you can't be serious? Can you conscientiously believe that your talent has sufficed to raise you so rapidly to the point you have attained in life; that it has given you all you possess:

The Confidences of an Academic Coat

honours, position, fame, fortune? Do you really think that possible, Guillardin? Examine yourself, my dear friend, before answering; go down, far, far down, into your inmost conscience. Now, answer me? Don't you see you dare not?"

"And yet," stammered Guillardin, with comical hesitation, "I've.... I've worked a great deal."

"Oh yes, a great deal, you have fagged tremendously. You are a toiler, a drudge, you knock off a great deal of work. You count your task by the hour, like a cabdriver. But the spark, my dear boy, which like a golden bee flits through the brain of the true artist, and emits from its wings both light and music, when has it ever visited you? Not once, and you are well aware of it. It has always frightened you, that divine little bee! And yet it is this only that gives real talent. Ah! I know many who also work, but very differently from you, with all the anxiety and fever of sincere research, and yet who will never reach the point you have attained. Look here, acknowledge this much, now we are alone. Your one talent has been marrying a pretty woman."

"Monsieur!" interrupted Guillardin, turning purple.

The voice proceeded unchanged:

The Confidences of an Academic Coat

"Ah well! This burst of indignation is a good sign. It proves to me what all the world knows indeed; that you are certainly more fool than knave. Come, come, you need not roll such furious eyes at me. In the first place, if you touch me, if you make the least crease or tear in me, it will be impossible to go to reception today, and then, what will Madame Guillardin say? For after all, it is to her that all the glory of this great day is due. It is she whom the five Academies are about to receive, and I can assure you that if I appeared at the *Institut* on her pretty person, still so elegant and slender notwithstanding her age, I should cut a very different figure than with you. Confound it, Monsieur Guillardin, we must look facts in the face! You owe everything to that woman; everything, your house, your forty thousand francs (sixteen hundred pounds) a year, your cross of the Legion of Honour, your laurels, your medals."

And with the gesture of a one-armed man, the green coat, with its empty embroidered sleeve, pointed out to the unfortunate sculptor the glorious insignia hung up on the walls of his alcove. Then, as though wishing the better to torment his victim, to assume every aspect, and every attitude, the cruel coat drew nearer the fire, and leaning

The Confidences of an Academic Coat

forward on his armchair with a little old-fashioned and confidential air, he spoke familiarly, in the tone of a long-established intimacy:

"Come, old boy, what I've said seems to upset you. Yet it is better you should know what everybody is aware of. And who could tell you better than your own coat? Let us reason a little. What had you when you married? Nothing. What did your wife bring you? Nothing. Then how do you explain your present fortune? You are going to repeat again that you have worked very hard. But my poor friend, working day and night, with all the patronage and the orders from government which have certainly not been wanting to you since your marriage, you have never made more than fifteen thousand francs (six hundred pounds) a year. Can you for one moment suppose that was sufficient to keep up an establishment like yours? Remember that the beautiful Madame Guillardin has always been cited as a model of elegance, frequenting the richest society. Of course I am well aware that shut up as you were from morning till night in you studio, you never gave a thought to all this. You were satisfied with saying no to your friends: 'I have a wife who is a surprisingly skillful manager. With what I gain, she not only pays

The Confidences of an Academic Coat

our expenses, but manages also to put by money.' It was you who were surprising, poor man! The truth was that you had married one of those pretty little unscrupulous creatures of which Paris is full, an ambitious flirt, serious in what concerned your interests and unprejudiced in regard of her own, knowing how to reconcile your affairs and her pleasures. The life of these women, my dear fellow, resembles a dance programme in which sums would be placed side by side with the dancers' names. Yours reasoned in the following manner: 'My husband has no talent, no fortune, no good looks either; but he is an excellent man, good-natured, credulous, as little in the way as possible. Provided he leaves me free to amuse myself as I choose, I can undertake to give him all he lacks!' And from that day forth, money, orders, decorations from all countries kept pouring in upon your studio, with their pretty metallic sound and their many-coloured ribbons. Look at the row on my lapel. Then one fine morning, Madame was seized with the fancy—a fancy of beauty on the wane—to be the wife of an Academician, and it is her delicately gloved hand that has opened before you one by one all the doors of the sanctuary. Ah! my poor old fellow, your colleagues alone can tell you what all these green palms have cost you!"

The Confidences of an Academic Coat

"You lie, you lie!" screamed Guillardin, half choked by indignation.

"Ah no! my old friend, indeed I do not lie. You need only to look around you presently, when you enter the reception hall. You will see a malicious gleam in every eye, a smile at the corner of every lip, while they will whisper as you pass by: 'Here is the beautiful Madame Guillardin's husband.' For you will never be anything else in life, my dear fellow, but the husband of a pretty woman."

This time, Guillardin could bear it no longer. Pale with rage, he bounded forward, to seize and dash into the fire, after first tearing from it the pretty green palm wreath, this insolent and raving coat; but a door opens and a well-known voice, tinged with a mixture of contempt and mild condescension, opportunely awakes him from his horrible nightmare:

"Oh! that is just like you, asleep at the corner of the fire on such an important day!"

And Madame Guillardin stands before him, tall and still handsome, although rather too imposing with her almost natural pink complexion, her powdered hair, and the exaggerated brilliancy of her painted eyes. With the gesture of the superior woman, she takes up the green-palmed coat, and briskly with a little smile, helps her husband

The Confidences of an Academic Coat

to don it; while he, poor man, still trembling with the horrors of his nightmare, draws a deep sigh of relief and thinks to himself: "Thank goodness! It was a dream!"